Bennet

# Bennet

## STORIES OF HUMOR, GRACE, AND HOPE

EUGENIA A. GAMBLE

Bridge Resources
Louisville, Kentucky

Unless otherwise noted, Scripture quotations are from the New Revised Standard Version of the Bible, copyright © 1989 by the Division of Christian Education of the National Council of the Churches of Christ in the U.S.A. Used by permission.

Every effort has been made to trace copyrights on the materials included in this book. If any copyrighted material has nevertheless been included without permission and due acknowledgment, proper credit will be inserted in future printings after notice has been received.

*Edited by Janice E. Catron*

*Book and cover design by Anthony Feltner*

*Cover illustration by John Foster*

*First edition*

Published by Bridge Resources

Louisville, Kentucky

Web site address: http://www.bridgeresources.org

PRINTED IN THE UNITED STATES OF AMERICA

98 99 00 01 02 03 04 05 06 07 — 10 9 8 7 6 5 4 3 2 1

**Library of Congress Cataloging-in-Publication Data**

Gamble, Eugenia, date.
    Bennet / Eugenia Gamble. — 1st ed.
      p. cm.
    ISBN 1-57895-065-1
      1. United States—Social life and customs—20th century—Fiction.
    2. Boys—United States—Fiction. I. Title.
    PS3557.A4486B46 1998
    813´.54—dc21

                                           98-33773

*To the members and friends of the First Presbyterian Church
in Englewood, Colorado, where Bennet was "born," and to my friend
Janice Catron, who was intent on setting him loose on the world.*

# Contents

# 1

# Bennet's Christmas Eve

Once upon a time in a land far away, somewhere to the South and a little to the East, a small boy named Bennet awoke with a scratchy throat.

"Rats," Bennet said, rubbing his throat, swallowing a couple of times, and taking a few deep breaths to test the situation.

This was nothing new for Bennet. He had spent much of his young life in oxygen tents and on antibiotics and steroids. Invariably, the winter chill brought tinsel and carols—and an upper respiratory infection that drained the color from his mother's face and sent Bennet to bed with honeyed tea and a stack of Spider Man comic books.

Winter was his favorite season, the cruelty notwithstanding. He always felt close to the edge in winter, and he always got a part in the church's Christmas pageant. Nine times out of ten, Keith Adams got to play the part because Bennet was sick, but Bennet always got cast. He got to attend at least some of the rehearsals and, along with the other boys, would terrorize the little angels.

He could cope with Mary, even when Genevieve Farmer—who thought she was better than everybody—got the part, but that swarm of little angels in white gauze costumes and tinsel crowns made him sick. What kind of self-respecting angel would fly around like that in this day and age?

It was Christmas Eve. As he stumbled out of bed to go and break the news to his sleeping mother, Bennet knew that Keith Adams would be the lead shepherd again. He raised his arm and practiced pointing to the heavens one last time, then walked through the bathroom into his mother's dim bedroom.

The sun was creeping its gray winter way up, and so was Bennet's mom, Laura.

"Mom," Bennet squeaked, as he stood barefoot on the hardwood floor by her bed.

"Oh, honey," she said, her hand instinctively reaching from under the covers to feel his forehead. "Oh, honey," she said again. "You run back to bed and cover up warm. I'll call the doctor and make you some honey tea and cinnamon toast, okay?"

"Okay," he said, as he turned to head back to his bedroom. "Will you give Keith a call? The pageant is tonight."

"Sure, honey," his mom said, switching on the light and reaching for the phone.

From his bed, Bennet could hear his mom on the phone. "Vernon? It's Laura. Bennet is down again. Well, yesterday he seemed a little sluggish, but he swore he was okay. He spent most of the day in one of Fred's old bathrobes, pointing to the sky and saying, 'I got you this time, Keith Adams.' Yes. The pageant. I know, but this morning he's burning up. Thank you. I'll keep him in. Yes, I'll tell Bennet you'll stop by after you get out of surgery. Merry Christmas, and thanks again, Vernon. I don't know what we would do without you. Bye."

Bennet heard his mom fumble for her slippers and dial the phone again. "Mr. Everett, this is Laura. Mr. Everett, is there any way you could get by without me today? Bennet is sick again. I know it's Christmas Eve, but he's burning up. I just don't want to leave him. Of course I want my job, Mr. Everett. I'll try to find someone, but if I can't, I can't leave a sick child alone." She hung up without saying good-bye.

More dialing. "JoAnn, this is Laura. Oh, you too. Listen, Bennet's down again. Is there anyway you could sit with him for a while? I have to go to work. Oh, that would be great if Frances could come. Even just until noon. I'm sure I can get home at noon, if I can just go in now. Oh, thanks a million. Vernon is going to stop by later and take a look at him. Bye."

Bennet's mother hung up the phone, and Bennet could hear her making her way to the kitchen to make his tea and toast. He lay back on his pillow and closed his eyes. His eye sockets felt like someone was storing hot coals in them, and the familiar pull in his chest was growing. He tried to cough.

"Rats," was all he mumbled.

A few minutes later, his mom came in with juice and tea and cinnamon toast on a tray. "Honey, I've got to go to work this morning. Frances is going to come over and stay with you for a while. The drugstore is sending over some medicine. You take one pill right away. You remember how, don't you? Lots and lots of water."

"It's okay, Mom. I remember, and I don't need anybody to stay with me."

"I know, honey. I need someone to stay with you, okay?"

"Okay. Did you get Keith?"

"No. It's still early. I'll call from the store."

"Don't forget, and Mom, tell him if he wants to use the costume, he can."

"Okay, honey. Try to drink your tea and sleep a little more. I'll come and kiss you good-bye."

Bennet drank some of the tea. The steam seemed to loosen up his chest a little. He munched on the cinnamon toast and flipped through his newest Spider Man comic book. Before his mother left the house, Bennet was asleep.

He woke up an hour later. He could hear Frances in the living room, watching TV and talking on the phone. He stayed quiet. The last thing he needed was Frances in here, harassing him. Frances was a teenager in the worst sense of the word. She liked nothing better than tormenting him and using him to pick up boys.

"Poor Bennet," she would coo into the phone. "It must be so hard to be so sick and have absolutely no positive male role models in his life. I know. I know. Oh, you mean you wouldn't mind coming over and playing with him for a little while? You're such an angel [insert name of the week]."

Barf, Bennet thought. As long as she thought he was asleep, he was safe, but he was also bored. After all, how many times could Spider Man stick to the same ceiling without the glue coming off his boots?

Bennet began to play with the quilt his grandmother had made. His father's mother. He hadn't known her. He hadn't known his father either, really. He was so young when it all happened. He and his mom had not kept up with the rest of his dad's family. He knew there was a brother off somewhere and a great aunt so-and-so, but that was about it.

He loved the quilt, though. It was a little ragged, but hand-sewn from a dozen different fabrics and colors, all in squares and zigzags. Bennet would divide the quilt up into nations. Good nations were colors he liked, and evil empires were colors girls liked. Then he would plot his conquest, how he would conquer the world for right and decency. It would keep him occupied for a long time.

This morning, as he was plotting his peaceful takeover of the Pink Stink, a strange thing happened.

An angel appeared to Bennet, right there on the foot of the bed, with next-door-neighbor Frances cooing into the phone in the other room.

"Hark," the angel said.

"Whoa!" Bennet said.

"Hark," the angel said again. "Hark—that's what angels say when they first show up in a place."

"Well, what does it mean?" Bennet asked.

"I have no idea," the angel said. "I don't make the rules. I just go where I'm sent and say what I am sent to say."

"So let me get this straight. You were sent here today, of all days, to tell me 'Hark'? Get out of here. You're no angel. You're a figment of my imagination," Bennet said huffily.

"Nope," the angel said. "I'm an angel all right. A messenger of God."

"Well, you don't look like an angel," Bennet said.

That was for sure. The angel that sat at the foot of Bennet's bed looked a lot like a donkey. It was shaped like a donkey—except that instead of ears he had wings—and his body was covered with feathers.

"Angels look like a lot of different things," the angel said. "Angels always come in the form in which they can be received."

"Well, I'm allergic to feathers," Bennet said.

"Not these feathers," the angel responded. "My feathers are made of healing herbs. Nobody is allergic to them. See," the angel said, sticking a tufted hoof under Bennet's nose, and grazing Bennet's upper lip. Bennet was shocked that the angel had touched him, and he was silent.

The angel continued, "Bennet Boling Lawson, I have a message for you."

Bennet gulped.

"What, I'm going to have a baby?"

"No," the angel snorted. "Not exactly."

Suddenly the angel seemed to get all nostalgic. "That was one of my great moments," he said. "Mary was such a feisty little thing—so sure of herself, so willing to take on anything."

"You're not Gabriel!" Bennet thundered.

"Oh?" the angel said. "I think so."

"Where does it say in the Bible that the angel Gabriel was a feathered . . . donkey?"

"I told you already. I come in the ways I can be received. This is my favorite, though. I went like this to the stable that night. Only God made me check my wings at the door on account of the innkeeper being a nervous sort. And Joseph wasn't coping all that well at this point. Joseph was a good boy, don't get me wrong, but when it got right down to Mary having this baby, he got a little worked up again. That's why he took so long getting the midwife. He was having a little trouble with his 'coper.' People do that when their lives don't go the way they've planned."

"Wait a minute," Bennet interrupted. "You were there? You were there when Jesus was born?"

"Why, certainly," the angel said. "I wouldn't have missed it, would you? God had to make sure that nothing went wrong with the delivery—human freedom and all, you know—so that's why he sent all of us."

"All of who?" Bennet asked.

"The animals. We were all angels, all on a mission. Some quietly and inconspicuously moved clean straw toward Mary, when Joseph and the midwife were occupied. Some stood in front of the cave door to block the draft. After the baby was born, I stood right next to the manger to keep him warm, while Joseph just cradled Mary in his arms while she slept. Joseph never slept. He just rocked Mary in his arms and stared at the baby."

Suddenly, all around the angel, Bennet could see the long-ago scene played out right on the nations of his grandmother's quilt. He saw the sheep, blocking the door; the small ox, pushing straw with its muzzle; and the donkey, guarding the baby while the mother dozed and the startled father stared.

He could see outside the cave: the bustle of the busy city, full of strangers and foreigners, looking for something to feel like home. He could hear the hassled voices of the innkeeper and his staff, trying to serve the arrogant out-of-towners.

In the sky, he could see a point of light, somewhere in the universe. It looked like a laugh would look, if you could paint its energy silver. He could see the ragtag band of hooligan shepherds, shaking their heads and covering their eyes from the bright, white light of God's laugh in the sky. He could see them gathering their scraggly flocks together and heading in the direction of the cave.

On the other side of the world, fancy men in velvet robes took out long glasses to examine the sky and then began to pack for a lengthy journey, leaving their pondering families at home.

All of this Bennet could see in the silver shadow the angel cast on his grandmother's quilt. "Wow!" Bennet said, breathing in a little too deeply and feeling the slicing pain in his lungs. "Awesome!" he whispered, lying back against his pillow and never taking his eyes from the unusual angel at the foot of his bed.

"You said you had a message for me?" Bennet said tentatively.

"You bet I did, Bennet. Just like that night so long ago, God sent me here to guard your cradle—to make sure that nothing goes wrong, to make sure that, come what may, you will be able to be all that God has dreamed for you. I have good news for you, Bennet Boling Lawson. Unto you this night is born a Savior. One who comes to confirm all your hopes, one who comes to bring you the salvation of your God, one who is called Christ the Lord . . . Immanuel . . . God with *you*. So from this day forevermore, you can be sure that when you are sick and when you are well, when you fail and when you succeed, when you hurt and when you rejoice, the things that lie ahead are more wonderful than you can dream, because your God has come to be with you."

"Gloria," Bennet said a little weakly, with hot, feverish tears running down his small cheeks.

"Gloria in Excelsis!" the angel said.

"Deo," Bennet said, and the angel was gone.

For a moment Bennet was very still. He tested his breathing for a predictable miracle. It was still labored and he was still hot, but the room was filled with the scent of healing herbs. A silver light fell all across his grandmother's quilt.

At that moment there was a tentative knock on the door and Frances stuck her head in. "Bennet? Keith Adams is here to get the costume, okay?"

"Send him in," Bennet said with a smile. "Maybe I have some tips for him."

# 2

# Bennet's Christmas Day

Once upon a time in a land far away, somewhere to the South and a little to the East, a small boy named Bennet slept late on Christmas Day. Most of his friends had been up before dawn, tearing through their houses, tossing brightly colored paper into the air in ecstasy. Most of their toys were broken before Bennet rallied from his fitful sleep to peek through the cracks in his bedroom door at the lights twinkling on the tree.

Bennet's mom, Laura, had been up early, dressing and preparing the great turkey for the relatives, who were even now winding their bleary way down Highway 80 with the smell of his mom's dressing tickling their noses.

Bennet could smell the first faint smells of the roasting bird, fat with cornbread and onions. Bennet licked his lips. He was in no rush to get up. Partly because he had been so sick, and the night of labored breathing had left him weak. Mostly because yesterday morning he again had been forced to relinquish his part as lead shepherd in the Christmas Eve pageant, because of yet another respiratory infection. Bennet had been visited by the angel Gabriel in the form of a donkey, with wings for ears and feathers for fur. Since that angelic visitation, Bennet had not been in a hurry about much of anything.

Gabriel had sat with Bennet, right on the foot of the bed, on his grandmother's quilt, and told him all about that night in the stable. He had shown him the scene—how the candlelight reflected off the cave walls, and how all the animals in the stable had really been angels on a mission from God to make sure nothing went wrong.

After the pageant, his mother's friend Midge had stopped by the house to bring him some molasses cookies made from his Aunt Suzy's antique recipe. Midge had told him how much the church people and the other children had missed him in the pageant. She said that his bathrobe shepherd's costume had given a stellar performance, even if it was on the back of Keith Adams. Bennet was appreciative, but unimpressed. All those little girls in gauze angel costumes simply couldn't hold his interest.

Bennet had asked his mom to bring him the little German crèche, which always sat on the end table by the tree from Christmas Eve through Three Kings' Day. He had set and reset the crèche in various positions on his grandmother's quilt, trying to remember it exactly the way that Gabriel had shown him. Finally, in exhaustion and fever, he had fallen asleep with the baby Jesus and the animals clutched in his small fist. They were still there. He was certain, although he had not yet unclenched his small fist.

There was a knock on his bedroom door and his mom's smiling face peeked in.

"Ho, ho, ho, sleepyhead." She had cinnamon toast and tea on a tray. "Merry Christmas, honey. Do you feel like bundling up on the sofa or shall I bring your presents in here?"

"I think I'll come out for a while, Mom. I'm feeling better." This was almost true.

His mother crinkled her brow in response.

"Relax, Mom," Bennet said. "It's running its course." Bennet was a practical child and had heard this phrase whispered by the doctor to his mom on numerous occasions.

His mother smiled. "Eat some toast to tide you over first. That infernal bird probably won't be ready until two. The thing is enormous. I had to tie its wings together to even get it into the oven. Charlotte and Hugh and the kids will probably be here in about an hour." His mother glanced anxiously at her watch. "Well, they'll just have to wait." She laid out Bennet's fuzzy bathrobe and slippers across the foot of the bed. "Don't you dare get out of that bed without your slippers, young man," she said with a smile as she went back to the kitchen to worry about the bird.

Bennet munched on the toast for a minute. Then he tied the pieces of the crèche in his napkin, pulled on his robe and slippers, stuffed the napkin in his pocket, and headed for the sofa, dragging his grandmother's quilt behind him.

He took some time to decide just where to place himself on the sofa. After all, those wild cousins of his would be here soon, and if he was not firmly entrenched in the choice seat, he knew he would be jostled right out of view of the tree.

What a tree it was! Bennet and his mom usually had a small tabletop tree, but this year one of his mother's friends from the church had cut one for them from his land. It was a fat and prosperous-looking cedar tree, so tall that the tree angel had to sit on the coffee table instead of on top of the tree. The lights went nearly to the top, though, and they twinkled like Mardi Gras stars, even in the clear December sunshine streaming through the windows.

Bennet was still relishing the tree and clutching the crèche, when the blue Taurus station wagon pulled into the driveway. His cousins, Lloyd and Ginny, piled out, leaving their parents to haul in brightly wrapped boxes and the annual bottle of champagne.

Ginny was deceptively dressed in a sweet green velvet dress with a lace collar, exactly like her mother's. Lloyd had on a tiny blue suit and tie, and looked for all the world like a Brooks Brothers' elf. That won't last long, Bennet thought, as Lloyd and Ginny tumbled through the front door yelling, "Merry Christmas! Merry Christmas!"

"Ho! Ho! Ho!" Bennet said.

Lloyd and Ginny came to the couch and began to perch on top of Bennet to get the best view of the tree. "You sick again?" Ginny asked, more curious than concerned.

"A little," Bennet replied. Bennet never quite knew what to make of Lloyd and Ginny. Their father was a prosperous attorney, and Lloyd and Ginny seemed to take their prosperity for granted, vacillating from disdain to fascination at the rickety old house that Bennet and his mother lived in.

It had been Bennet's grandmother's house, and grand in its day. It was a three-story Victorian, and a bear to heat. The upper two floors had long since been closed off, and Bennet and his mom had made a cozy little nest for themselves on the ground floor.

"Did you get to be in the pageant this year?" Lloyd asked Bennet.

Bennet just shook his head.

"I did," Ginny chimed in. "I got to be one of the angels at our church.

I wore a beautiful white gown and a golden crown."

Barf, Bennet thought. "That's nice, Ginny," Bennet said.

By this time, Charlotte and Bennet's mother were hugging and squealing, and Hugh was pumping Bennet's hand and calling him "old man."

Christmas Day made Bennet feel like an old man all right. It was just so different from all the other days. It was fun, but something was always under the surface. It was so full of the end of anticipation. There was always tomorrow waiting.

Bennet's mom came up behind him and gave him a hug. Her smile was as pure and true as a child's, and it gave Bennet the will to be patient.

"Hugh, will you be Santa this year or is it Lloyd's turn?" his mom asked, wiping her hands on her apron and perching next to Bennet on the sofa.

"I think its Lloyd's day, Laura," Hugh said, leaning back against the bookcase and tapping at his pipe. Hugh never smoked around Bennet, but he played with his pipe a lot.

"Okay, Lloyd, you know what to do. Just pile the presents up around the person they go to, and then we open them one at a time so everybody can see. Pile mine up over here. I'll have to be running back and forth to the kitchen, you know," Bennet's mom said with excitement. She loved Christmas Day. It made her feel like a child. It was so different from all the other days, full of the memories of wonderful yesterdays and the satisfaction of bringing joy to others.

Lloyd distributed the gifts in record time, and the unwrapping proceeded without a hitch. Bennet's mom got a silk nightgown from her sister, a colorful scarf from Lloyd, a sweater with reindeer doing the polka from Hugh, and a stuffed elf from Ginny.

Bennet fared well, too. Most special of all his gifts—in a box just marked "Bennet"—was a crèche of his very own, bigger than the little one he had clutched in his hand all night. It was Italian, made of terra cotta, and had finely molded animals of every description, together with worthy-looking shepherds and kings (but no angel). Bennet was delighted.

Bennet's mom knit her brow. "There is no tag, and I can't remember who dropped the box by. Now we don't know who to thank."

Bennet thought he knew who it might be, but he kept it to himself.

About the time that Bennet's mom was unwrapping the worsted-wool suit that Hugh had picked out for her from Lord & Taylor's, there was a knock at the door.

*Bennet: Stories of Humor, Grace, and Hope*

Lloyd went to answer it. On the porch stood a man about Hugh's age wearing a flannel shirt. In one hand he was holding a half-empty bag of Florida oranges, tied closed with rickrack, and, in the other hand, what appeared to be his laundry in a plastic garbage sack.

"Hi, son. You must be Bennet," the man said.

"No. I'm Lloyd," the child answered, planting his feet firmly, as he had seen his father do, when standing off door-to-door salesmen.

"Oh," the man said. "Isn't this still the Lawson residence?"

"Mom," Lloyd called over his shoulder, but his mother and father were already behind him. Ginny and Bennet's mom were in the kitchen, checking the bird.

Charlotte's face went white. "George," was all she said.

"Aren't you going to invite me in, Charlotte? It is Christmas, you know," the man said with a grin. He was enjoying her discomfort.

Hugh chimed in, "I don't think that's such a great idea, George. Laura's been through a lot lately and Bennet is sick again . . ."

"George?" It was Bennet's mom, coming up behind them to see what was going on. Her face was set. The child that had laughed and played with the scarf and elf was nowhere to be found. "What a surprise. Won't you come in?"

Hugh and Charlotte backed away from the door in startled dismay. Bennet's mom didn't look at either one of them. She didn't look at George either.

"I brought you some oranges," George said.

"Thank you," Bennet's mom said. "I'll just put them in the fridge."

Charlotte followed her into the kitchen. "Are you crazy?" Charlotte fumed. She was obviously livid. "Are you crazy? Haven't you suffered enough at the hands of those Lawson men? And what about Bennet? Is that the kind of influence you want him exposed to?"

Bennet's mom remained steely calm. "Charlotte, I didn't invite George here, but he is Bennet's uncle. What do you want me to do, slam the door in his face on Christmas Day? We're living in his mother's house, you know. We don't own it. We don't even rent it. If any of the Lawsons wanted to claim it, they could, and then where would Bennet and I be?"

"Well, for one thing, you could come to the city with us and get out of this godforsaken little slum. Hugh could get you a job with his firm and you could get some decent medical care for Bennet."

"Bennet has decent medical care, Charlotte, and this is not a slum. It is our home, and you, lest you forget, are a guest in it," Bennet's mom said, stabbing at the dressing in the electric frying pan. She took a very deep breath. "Charlotte," she said more gently, "this is my home. My friends are in this town, and my church. Bennet was born here. Do the doctors in the city still make house calls? Vernon does, any time of the day or night. If Bennet needs anything special, Vernon sees to it for us. What would happen to him in the city? The kids would call him names. He'd be so isolated. Here the kids have known him since he was born. They all know he has asthma. They all know it's bad, but to them it's just a part of Bennet, like green eyes and red hair. Is that how it would be in the city?"

"Well, it could be," Charlotte insisted, slowed down but undeterred. "Look at us. That man has been in this house for five minutes and we are already at each other's throats. He wants something. I just know he does, and you can bet it's not something good."

Bennet's mom put down the wooden spoon and put her arm around Charlotte. "Let's just make the best of it. Who knows, maybe he's changed. Help me with this bird, will you? It weighs a ton."

"It's a good thing," Charlotte said sulkily. "George doesn't look like he's eaten for a while."

"No," Laura said. She was quiet for a moment. "He looks like Fred, doesn't he?"

Meanwhile in the living room, George had perched himself on the foot of Bennet's sofa, thrown his arm casually over the back, and begun to chat with Bennet like they were long lost friends.

"So how's tricks, Bennet? You remember your old Uncle George, don't you?"

Bennet wasn't sure. He wasn't sure if he remembered George or just the stories of George. In either case, he remembered people's responses to those stories—the stiffening of their backs, the blankness that came over his mother's face. Over George's shoulder, Bennet could see Charlotte setting another place at the table.

George was rambling on about the highway to Fort Lauderdale and how people just weren't as friendly as they used to be, when Bennet's mom came into the room. "Dinner is served, everybody. Will you be able to stay, George?"

"Of course, Laura. I've come a long way for one of your turkey dinners."

Everyone rose quietly but Bennet. Lloyd and Ginny hadn't said a word since George got there. Ginny was clinging to her father's leg and peeping sheepishly from behind it.

"Mom," Bennet asked. "May I come to the table?"

His mom automatically put her hand on his forehead. "Are you sure you feel like it, honey?" Bennet nodded. "Okay, then. But it's back to bed right after, okay?"

"Okay," Bennet said, positioning himself next to his Uncle George.

The conversation around the table was stilted—football, the Camellia Show, the Benefit Art Show that Charlotte was chairing.

Bennet began to wonder why his new crèche had no angel. "I wonder . . ." Bennet mumbled, as he absently lined his English peas on his knife.

"What's that, Bennet?" his Uncle Hugh asked, obviously hoping for some help with the conversation.

"Eat your peas with a fork, please," his mother chastised.

Bennet didn't hear either one of them. Suddenly, all Bennet could hear was silence—a great and noble and holy silence, a silence he knew was for his ears only. Suddenly, the smells of the dinner were taken over by the sweet smell of healing herbs. His upper lip began to tremble and itch where Gabriel had touched it the day before.

I wonder, Bennet thought to himself. I wonder, if you touched my lip so that when you left, I would speak? Is that it, Gabriel? Am I the form your message can be received in today?

It seemed as if the silence grew wider and deeper, and Bennet felt that he was in a whole different universe from the strained universe of the Christmas table. He knew that he was still eating his meal, but he couldn't taste a thing. Something else was filling his mouth—not food or drink, but a message. He knew the angel had come to him the day before to tell him that God loved him and would always be with him. Maybe he was supposed to be that angel for Uncle George. "Is that it, Gabriel?" Bennet whispered, and he thought he heard the tinkling of the bells that Gabriel had worn on his collar.

Bennet gulped. The tension had grown around the table, during Bennet's reverie. Hugh was red-faced and sputtering, and George was heatedly saying something about the only good lawyer being a dead lawyer. Suddenly, Hugh jumped back from the table and began to take off his coat.

George looked startled. Charlotte looked horrified. Bennet's mom just looked tired. Ginny screamed and left the table, while Lloyd just said, "Dad. Dad. Don't."

"Why do you think God sent you here today, Uncle George?" Bennet asked quietly, all eyes suddenly on him.

George looked at Bennet, all the bluster gone from him. "Well, Bennet, this is my home. Your dad and I grew up in this house. When we were little fellas, we always had a big tree right where you and your mama have yours. But we were stupid, Bennet. We were bonehead stupid, and we made some bad mistakes. Mistakes so bad that we had to leave everything we cared for behind—this place, you, your mama, and your grandmama. We couldn't fix what we had done, even if we tried. We always wanted to come home, but your daddy died before he could get back to you. Your daddy had a present for you, Bennet. Something he made me promise to give to you as quick as I could. I promised him I would. I've been in jail, Bennet, and I couldn't get here until now."

"What kind of present?" Bennet asked.

"Here," George reached into the pocket of his jeans and brought out a wrinkled envelope and handed it to the feverish little boy. "It's a deed, Bennet. The deed to this house. Your daddy wanted you to have it—you and your mama. He wanted you to always know that no matter what happened, you would have a home. Your Uncle Hugh will have to fix it up all legal for you."

"Oh, George," Bennet's mom said, her eyes wide and damp, her hand covering her mouth.

Bennet opened the envelope and pulled out the creased document. He couldn't understand the words, but something made him lift the paper to his nose. Bennet didn't remember his father, but there was something familiar about the smell, just a hint of something he knew or almost knew.

"Welcome home, Uncle George," Bennet said softly.

The rest of the meal passed quietly, except when the applause rang out over the steaming apple dumpling and hard sauce. The tension was still there, but somehow it had been tempered a little with sadness and hope, regret and longing, and a quiet kind of awe.

After the meal, while Charlotte was helping Bennet's mom with the dishes, Ginny was sacked out under the tree, and Hugh was helping Lloyd assemble some battle toy, George tucked Bennet back under the quilt his mother had made for his nephew. He built up the fire a little.

"Do you want to see my crèche, Uncle George?" Bennet asked a little weakly. He was getting awfully tired.

"Sure, Bennet," George said and sat down on the floor by the sofa.

"Well," Bennet said. "I'm sure you know the story, right? Mary had the baby Jesus in a stable in Bethlehem, but the part that may surprise you is that all the animals were angels. Now the really important part is that they were sent to make sure that nothing went wrong, you know . . ."

"What's that smell? Do you smell it? It smells like an herb garden," George said looking around.

Bennet felt his lip twitch, "Uncle George?"

"Yes, Bennet."

"I don't care what happened, and I don't think God does either. We're both just glad you're home." Bennet was quiet for a moment, captured by the beauty of the tree and the way the lights twinkled on George's faded shirt.

"Merry Christmas, Uncle George," Bennet said and laid his head back on the pillow.

"Merry Christmas, sport."

# 3

# Bennet and the
# Change in Plans

Once upon a time in a land far away, somewhere to the South and a little to
the East, a small boy named Bennet missed church on Super Bowl Sunday.
This was not the way he had planned it yesterday. He and his best friend,
Harve Melton, had sat for hours on the drafty hardwood floors of Harve's
front hall, lining up marbles in various configurations of the Redskins and
the Bills. They had hoped for the Broncos and the Saints. They were still of
an age where, no matter what they said or yelled during the game, whoever
won was their all-time favorite team.

The plan had been for them to dash home after church. Reverend
Tucker had promised one and all that she would keep the service short and
pray for their divided hearts. The plan had been to make a break for it,
maybe during the final hymn, if they could get away with it. They'd run the
three blocks to Harve's house where Harve's mother, Mary Margaret, would
have sandwiches in the refrigerator and cookies shaped like footballs under
three layers of plastic on the counter. Then, they would set everything out,
be perched on the sofa, and halfway through their second sandwiches by the

time Big Harve and Mary Margaret got home to join them.

Bennet had wheezed a few times on Saturday, but never in front of an adult. He thought that he was home free, until about three o'clock in the morning. He awakened with the familiar gasps and the leaden feeling in his chest that he knew signaled the resurgence of a pesky upper respiratory infection that had dogged him since Christmas Eve.

It had been a bad one this year. On the day before Epiphany, the local doctor had arrived at the house in his long, black Cadillac to pick up Bennet, his mother Laura, and her sister Charlotte. He wrapped Bennet in his grandmother's quilt, and drove them the five hours to the Ocshner Clinic in New Orleans.

Bennet had liked the idea of being in New Orleans for Three Kings' Day. It was like a mini-Mardi Gras in the French Quarter, with people dressed up like animals and kings, throwing candy and shaking pole puppets. The angel Gabriel had, unbeknownst to Bennet's mom, visited him on Christmas Eve in the form of a donkey, with brown feathers made of healing herbs for fur and wings for ears. Bennet had decided there was a good chance that he would run into Gabriel again in New Orleans.

He had not. On the way home, he decided that, in fact, the wise men from the East had been there, although he had not seen them personally. He knew this because the oxygen machine, which pumped the finely misted medicine down deep into his scarred lungs, could have been nothing other than myrrh. It was too precious and wonderful. Only something brought by the wisest men in the world and consecrated at the cradle of Christ could feel that good.

With Bennet's lungs loosened and everybody's spirits high, the doctor had driven them all through the French Quarter the next day to see the parade and to have breakfast at Brennan's before heading home.

Bennet had felt fine for two weeks, but his fever never completely broke. Last night, the infection took another leap, and he knew that it was three or four more days of antibiotics, cinnamon toast, and Spider Man comic books for him.

The worst part was waking up his mother. Bennet's lungs scared her to death. Although she gathered every bit of her strength to keep from showing it, Bennet could see her small frame weaken every time he woke her with his rattling breath and croupy cough. She had taken it pretty well this time, though. It was Sunday, and she didn't have to worry about work or a baby-sitter.

Bennet's mom did hate to miss church, though. After she had taken Bennet's temperature, fixed him cinnamon toast and orange juice, fluffed his pillow, and pulled his grandmother's quilt up to his nose three times, she had wandered out into the living room and began flipping channels on the TV in the vain attempt to find a televised service that she could tolerate. Every now and then Bennet would hear her say, "Oh, for crying out loud," and flip the channel in disgust.

At thirty-four, Bennet's mom was already a matriarch of the church. She had been baptized there at six weeks old, becoming a youth elder in high school and a Sunday school teacher through all the dark days with Bennet's father. The church had always been there for his mom. She needed the words of her faith, articulated in the familiar rolling language of Reverend Tucker and the others, whose lives and stories she shared.

"Lord, have mercy," Bennet heard her sputter. Then he heard her toss the remote on the sofa and walk to his door. She peeked in, "Need anything, honey?"

"No, Mom. Sorry about church."

"Oh, honey, don't think a thing of it," his mom said, coming to the bed and putting her arms around him. "I secretly enjoy my disgust. I always get something out of those shows in spite of myself, even if it's just an appreciation of our own little church. Want some tea?"

"No thanks, Mom. I think I'm going to sleep for a while now."

"Okay, sweetie. I'll be right in the other room, if you need me." She pulled the quilt up to his nose again and tiptoed out of the room.

Bennet lay back on the pillows, pushed the quilt down under his armpits, and tried to sleep. He hoped that if he slept for a while, his mom would let him bundle up on the sofa later and watch the game. Bennet dozed.

He hadn't been asleep for long, when he heard the voice from the foot of the bed.

"Bennet Boling Lawson," the voice said, "I have a message for you."

Oh, no, Bennet thought. Not again. I'm going to have to have a baby for sure this time. He kept his eyes closed and held his breath, hoping this visitor would leave. There wasn't another sound. After a long time, when Bennet judged it to be safe, he opened one eye and peeked at the foot of the bed.

"Aha!" the visitor said.

"Rats," Bennet said, focusing on the strange old man with a white beard and musty-smelling wool coat, sitting cross-legged on the bed and leaning his chin on a cane.

Bennet was expecting maybe a Labrador retriever.

"Who are you?" Bennet asked.

"My name is Jeremiah," the visitor said.

"Not the prophet Jeremiah," Bennet said flatly. Bennet knew all about the prophet Jeremiah. He was one of Reverend Tucker's favorites, and she never missed an opportunity to talk about the strange old man she called the weeping prophet. Bennet remembered Reverend Tucker saying Jeremiah was not God's puppet, but God's person.

"At your service," the visitor said.

"Pleased to meet you," Bennet said. "I've heard a lot about you."

The old prophet sat back a little and looked away into space, as if scanning the ages for stories Bennet might have heard. "I've heard a lot about you too," the old man said after a moment. "You're very special to God, you know."

Bennet was startled and sat up a little. "That's really nice of you to say," he replied, trying to be polite. There was something in the way the prophet said those words that frightened Bennet. "You know, I really appreciate all this attention and all, being sick and everything, but you guys have got to cut this out! If my mom finds out that I have angels shaped like donkeys and dead prophets coming to my room on a regular basis, she'll send me to military school for sure."

"With those flat feet?" the visitor laughed. "Besides, she knows all about us."

Bennet was shocked. "She does?"

"Of course she does. Do you think your mother is stupid?"

Bennet shook his head.

"We just come to her in different ways—in her flower garden, in her women's group, in her books and prayers, in her Sunday school class, and in the choir anthems. Why do you think she gets so agitated when she's not at church in the winter? She finds most of her messengers from God there when nothing is blooming in her bulb garden."

"Oh," Bennet said. He had never considered that his mother might have visitations from God's messengers, too. It was a comforting thought, until it occurred to him that insanity often ran in families.

The old prophet leaned back and grinned at the small boy's thought process, which was racing across his feverish face.

"Bennet, you are tired. So I may as well get right to the point and let you get some rest."

Bennet nodded, but said nothing.

"Bennet Boling Lawson, God wants you to be a prophet."

"No way!" Bennet yelled, sure his mother would come running. Not a sound came from the living room. The visitor raised his eyebrows and said nothing. "It's too late," Bennet continued. "I have it all worked out already. I'm going to be an architect and design skyscrapers in Atlanta. I'm going to have a Chihuahua dog named Fred after my father, but I'll call him Myrtle or something, so it won't upset my mother. I'm going to have a family of my own and everything."

The visitor was silent, until he was sure Bennet had finished. "What's your point, Bennet?" the visitor asked.

"My point is that I think this is all a mistake. I don't want to do it. I'm just a little kid, and besides, whoever heard of a prophet who was an architect and had a Chihuahua dog? Besides, I'm sick a lot, you know. I mean, you can't ever tell when I might have to miss some special assignment or something. What if a city had to be destroyed right when I had a bad cold or something?" Bennet was running out of excuses. Weakly, he continued, "And what about seminary? I sure don't want to go to seminary. Reverend Tucker is talking all the time about what a concentration camp seminary was. Half the time she calls it 'cemetery' without even noticing. What about Harve? You know, my friend Harve Melton? He hasn't missed one day of Sunday school in three years. What about him?"

The old prophet thought for a moment. "Bennet, I think you've got the wrong idea on a couple of scores. First of all, who said anything about you not being an architect? All prophets aren't priests or ministers, you know. I myself was never a priest, although I was a priest's kid. I knew that was no life for me, but God wanted to use me in ordinary life. If you want to build skyscrapers and you can learn the math, you can do that and be a prophet too. About that Chihuahua dog—do you think that to answer God's call means you have to give up all the things in life that give you pleasure? Not true. Being a prophet just means being willing to speak the truth for God in whatever situation you find yourself. It's hard work. I won't say it's not. People have never liked the truth all that much, but you don't have to give up your dreams. Besides, it is a little-known fact, but true, that I myself had a Chihuahua dog named Eustice, who went with me everywhere. He was a good little dog, too."

"Now about this sickness thing, that is a great grief to God. God wants you to be well and strong, and is working very hard with your doctors and nurses to make that happen soon. You will be healthy one day, either in this life or the next. You don't have to wait to be perfect to be a prophet. One thing that is really funny about God is that sometimes it is our very weaknesses that allow God's power and truth to shine through us. Sometimes our hurts or our disabilities are really gifts in disguise that God can use to help other people. So, if you miss an assignment because you are sick, it might just be that the way you handle being sick is the message that someone needs most at that moment."

Bennet took a minute to contemplate all this, and the old prophet waited.

"But how will I know what to say?" Bennet asked after a time.

"Bennet, do you remember when you were baptized?"

"Of course not," Bennet said. "I was six weeks old, the size of a football, and had no hair."

"You had a little bit of hair," the visitor said, grinning. "Well, whether you remember it or not, it was a wonderful day. It was Reverend Tucker's first Sunday at the church, and nobody had put water in the font. She made the ushers go get a pitcher of water, while everybody sang a verse of "Amazing Grace." They got the water from the water fountain and it was ice cold. You screamed bloody murder. It was right then and there that God said, 'Those are the lungs that I want to proclaim my message.' "

Bennet smiled. He had heard the ice-water story, but was surprised it had made the circuit in heaven.

The visitor continued. "That's the only qualification you need. That's why you don't have to be afraid. When you were baptized, God's Spirit came right inside you, and that Spirit, if you will listen carefully, will give you the words you need to speak. It is that Spirit inside you that will tell you when the time comes to speak. It is that Spirit that will tell you, on your most painful days, when you have missed the opportunity to speak. Besides, Bennet, the word of prophecy is not that hard to grasp. It all finally boils down to three simple things. Your message to God's people, in one form or another, will always be one of those things. First, let God love you. Second, let God love others through you. And third, don't be confused about who God is in your life and who God is not. That's all I ever really said in all those wild oracles I preached. I tried to help my friends see the consequences of not letting that message into their lives and what it would cost them."

"Well, when you put it like that," Bennet said. "And if you're sure about the dog and all, I guess you can tell God I said okay."

"I'll let you do that for yourself, Bennet," the old prophet said. "Any questions?"

"When do I have to start?" Bennet asked, hoping it would not be until after the game.

"Well, Bennet, that is up to you. Do you know anyone who needs to let God love them?"

Bennet thought immediately of Mary Catherine Conrad. She was a little blond girl in his class whose parents were getting a divorce. Mary Catherine had been spending a lot of time crying behind the willow tree on the playground lately. "Well, there is Mary Catherine," Bennet said, timidly. "When Jana Woodruff told her she was sorry about her folks and all, Mary Catherine punched her in the nose and gave her a nosebleed."

"Well, Bennet, I never said it would be easy. You just ask God, and together you'll think of something."

Suddenly Bennet heard the doorbell ring, and he noticed that the room was filled with the scent of healing herbs, like when Gabriel had come on Christmas Eve.

"Is Gabriel here, too?" Bennet asked the visitor.

"Of course, Bennet. Gabriel is never far away from you. Only just a little farther away than God," the old man said, and was gone.

At that moment Bennet heard an excited knock at his bedroom door. His mom's smiling face peeked around the corner.

"Are you awake, sweetie?"

"Yeah, Mom. What is it?"

His mom entered the room. Her arms were crossed tightly across her chest. Her sweater was wiggling, and she was giggling like a child. Behind her, in the doorway, stood a couple of her friends from her women's group, whispering and giggling.

By the time she reached the bed, a tiny caramel-colored head that was mostly eyes and ears had popped out of the neck of her sweater. When she sat down next to Bennet, the tiny puppy jumped from the neck of her sweater and landed right on Bennet's chest and began licking his face furiously.

"Fr . . . Myrtle!" Bennet said, trying to harness the wild little creature.

"Do you like him, honey? He's eight weeks old today. Mary Margaret and Harve just brought him over from the kennel."

"He's great, Mom! Thanks. And Mom? Did you know that God and I love you?"

"Well, Bennet, God and I love you too," she said, hugging her son close. "Come on. Do you feel like bundling up on the sofa for a while? Harve is out there making a box for Myrtle, and it's almost time for the game to begin."

# 4

# Bennet and the Rabbit

Once upon a time in a land far away, somewhere to the South and a little to the East, a small boy named Bennet was halfheartedly poking through the tulips and the rice-paper plants for colored eggs, while his mother, Laura, and her best friend, Mary Margaret, paced, whispered, and dabbed at their eyes on the back porch. It didn't seem much like an Easter afternoon. Everything was blooming right on cue: the dogwoods and azaleas, the tulips and daffodils. Even the sky had cleared after a predawn storm, and the sun was turning the lingering raindrops into rainbow prisms. God was trying hard, but nobody seemed to notice.

Even Reverend Tucker, who loved Easter at least as much as she loved chocolate chip ice cream, had seemed a little off her mark this morning. At the sunrise service—which had to be held in the fellowship hall due to the storm—Wanda Williams, who was supposed to play Mary Magdalene, had been forced to drop out at the last minute with an uncontrollable bout of the hiccups. The service went ahead without her, with the Reverend Tucker reading her lines from behind a sheet and everybody staring at the empty space where Wanda should have stood. It was more of a morning for empty spaces than empty tombs anyway. So everybody thought, and nobody said.

It had been a hard week. On Monday, William Henderson, one of Bennet's classmates and the president of the fourth-grade youth fellowship, had been rushed to the hospital in Montgomery. William's leukemia had returned, and he had taken a sudden, terrible turn. The thought of that day had been in the back of the minds of William's friends for two years, but nobody ever spoke of it. It was just there, crouching behind the eyes every time anyone caught a glimpse of William's scruffy blond head racing after a ball on the playground or bobbing up and down when he thought he knew the answer to a question asked in class. The thought had been there for a moment, then blinked away. Unthinkable. Unacceptable. Untrue.

When William had first been diagnosed, he had gone for three months to St. Jude's Children's Hospital for experimental treatments. Reverend Tucker had borrowed a friend's van and taken the whole youth group up to Memphis to see him once. For weeks Bennet had dreamed about the blue hospital gowns with the little golden ducks on all the balding children. It had been a quiet trip. For a while after William came home, he had been fine, healthy, and active. His Cheshire-cat grin had almost dispelled the fears of his family and friends.

After Christmas, though, he had begun to look a little pale, to tire a little before the other boys. Last week he caught a nasty cold, and on Monday he was taken to the Montgomery hospital. On Thursday an ambulance came and got him to take him back to the local hospital, where he could be closer to his friends and family. The choir was rehearsing for the Good Friday service. Bennet and his best friend, Harve, were playing in the back of the church while their parents sang, when they heard the sound of the ambulance come near and then fade away. The choir members heard it, too, over the plaintive wail of the organ. It threw their timing off, taking breaths in at the wrong time and too deeply. Nobody said a word. They simply started over from the top.

"I'll bet that was William," Harve whispered.

"Yeah," Bennet said, kicking the pew in front of him.

William died on Holy Saturday. Bennet and his mother had been in the kitchen, dying Easter eggs, when the call came. The kitchen was filled with the smell of warm vinegar, a smell Bennet would forever associate with loss. William's mother told Bennet's mom that William had asked that Bennet and Harve be honorary pallbearers at the service, which would be at two o'clock Monday afternoon at the church. Mrs. Maddox, the school principal, had given permission for the whole class to attend the funeral, as long as each child had a signed permission slip. She would have a substitute teacher stay with the children who didn't wish to attend.

Bennet looked up from under a rice-paper leaf and saw his mother and her friend pacing and whispering. He knew they were discussing Mrs. Henderson's request. Bennet had not cried when his mother told him, at least not with tears. Something inside him had turned his tears off at the source. He wasn't sure what.

Bennet stood up and headed for the round flower bed in the middle of the yard. It was his mother's pride and joy. Each year she filled it with dozens of different bulbs—tulips, daffodils, and narcissus. She would pour over garden catalogs for months choosing the bulbs. Each year she would divide the bulbs and give some away to friends and neighbors, so there would always be room for new ones.

Bennet's mom always hid the golden egg in the round flower bed. It wasn't that she lacked imagination. She simply loved tradition. Bennet knelt at the edge of the bed, feeling the damp ground soak his knees, and began to search for the egg, plant by plant.

Suddenly, he saw something out of the corner of his eye, all pastels—yellow, pink, and lavender. He reached for it and jumped back.

"Whoa!" he said. The thing was soft, and it moved. Bennet separated the plants and leaned forward close to the ground. The egg wasn't an egg after all. It was a tiny pastel rabbit with a yellow body, lavender ears, and a pink fluffy tail. It was no bigger than Bennet's thumb, and its whiskers, like an iridescent fishing line, were twitching wildly.

"Bennet Boling Lawson," the rabbit said.

Bennet's hand flew to his head the way he had seen his mother's hand fly in the face of every unexplained shock of her life.

Oh, no. Not today, he thought. "Who are you?" he asked.

"It's me, Bennet. You know, your old friend, Gabriel," the rabbit answered with a tiny bow that almost got his tail caught in his ears.

The last time Bennet had seen Gabriel, the angel had appeared on Christmas Eve as a donkey, with healing herbs for fur and wings for ears.

"Oh, hello," Bennet said. "I didn't recognize you."

"Quite all right, my boy," the rabbit said, plopping his pink tail into the red mud. "Quite all right. So, how's it going, Bennet? You seem a little bummed out."

Bennet was momentarily taken aback. A thumb-sized pastel rabbit angel saying "bummed out" in the middle of his mother's flower garden was a bit of a shock. Bennet was expecting maybe a "hark" or a "lo" or a "behold," but "bummed out" seemed a little trendy for heaven. Bennet recovered.

"I guess I *am* a little bummed," the boy said. "My friend William died, did you hear?"

"Yes, Bennet. I heard," the rabbit said. "I know you are going to miss him a lot. I'm sorry."

"Yeah," Bennet said. He felt himself about to cry. It felt like the tears were creeping upward through his chest, but he stopped them. He was afraid that if he dripped on the rabbit, it would melt.

"Listen, Bennet," Gabriel said. "I won't keep you long. God just asked me to stop by and pay my respects . . . see if you need anything. Do you need anything?"

Bennet thought about this for a moment. He thought of a whole lot of things he had always wanted and none of them seemed very important. "I guess not. Oh, I don't know," he said, hanging his head.

"Well," the rabbit said, standing. "The boss just wanted me to tell you that everything is under control."

Bennet was silent.

"With William," the rabbit said. "Bennet, God is taking care of William."

"Well, it's a little late for that, don't you think?" Bennet snapped.

"No," replied the rabbit.

The boy and the rabbit spent a few minutes trying to out-silence each other. Finally, the rabbit said, "Bennet, did you hear what Reverend Tucker said this morning about Easter?"

"Yeah," Bennet said, trying to remember.

"About how Jesus died on the cross for us and then how God raised him on Easter morning, remember?"

"Yeah," Bennet said.

"Well, do you believe that, Bennet?" the rabbit asked.

"I guess so," Bennet said.

"Well, that's good," the rabbit said, sailing right past Bennet's uncertainty. "That's very good. You see, Jesus' resurrection is not just something that happened a long time ago and gives you an excuse to eat lots of candy and root around in your mother's flowers. No, siree," the rabbit said.

Bennet could tell that the rabbit was getting very worked up about this subject.

"You see, Jesus' resurrection is important because that's where your hope comes from when you need it, especially on days like this, when someone you love is gone. Bennet, do you know what hope is?"

"It's like a wish, isn't it?" Bennet answered.

"Not exactly, Bennet. Hope, for Christians, is much more than a wish. Hope is an assurance, a firm and binding promise from God. The hope, the firm promise that comes on Easter is a simple one, but a special one. Because Jesus lives on and on, we will too. This is the hope that comes from the resurrection."

Bennet stared blankly. He had heard all this before. The rabbit took a deep breath. "Bennet, it's not all over. It will never be all over. Not for William. Not for your dad. It will never be all over for your mom, and it never will be for you. *Different* is another story, but *over* is not a part of it."

Bennet looked at the rabbit. Suddenly the rabbit grinned a huge Cheshire-cat grin, from lavender ear to lavender ear, just like William's when he made a base hit or solved a math problem.

Bennet opened his mouth, "You, you look just like . . ."

"I know," the rabbit said. "William has been teaching me to smile properly. When I get the smile down, he said we could work on a few suggestions he has that might improve my batting average."

Bennet stared at the rabbit. The tears were up to his throat.

"Bennet Boling Lawson," the rabbit said. "Jesus Christ is risen. Don't ever forget that. Jesus Christ is risen. By the way, William says, 'Hi.' " With that, the scent of healing herbs overtook the smell of the flowers, and the rabbit was gone. In his place was the golden egg that Bennet's mother had worked for weeks to paint and cover with sequins.

"Alleluia," Bennet whispered as he picked up the egg. He stood up and began to run for the porch, where his mom and Mary Margaret were sipping tea with mint. The tears were pouring down his cheeks. His mom met him at the steps and put her arms around him. "Oh, honey," she said, patting him on the shoulder. "It will be all right."

"I know, Mom," Bennet said. "I really know."

*Bennet: Stories of Humor, Grace, and Hope*

# 5

# Bennet and the Gift

Once upon a time in a land far away, somewhere to the South and a little to the East, a small boy named Bennet was hiding behind the dossal curtain in the sanctuary of his church, trying hard not to move. It was the second day of vacation Bible school. Much to Bennet's chagrin, his mother, Laura—who was, Bennet believed, equipped with an incredible system of radar—had not believed him that morning at the breakfast table. Bennet, clutching his chest with his right hand and rolling his eyes back in his head, had said he thought he was having a heart attack and maybe he shouldn't go to vacation Bible school that day.

Even his little Chihuahua dog, Fred—named after his father, but called Myrtle so as not to upset his mother—had not believed him. The dog just sat there on the rag rug under the kitchen table, with his tiny head and enormous ears cocked to one side, and sighed. Bennet knew it was a pitiful performance. He didn't need an out-of-proportion Chihuahua dog critic to tell him that. He thought that he might at least get *some* credit for originality. After all, Bennet's mother was the dramatic type herself.

But alas, it was not to be so. His mom had simply looked at Bennet over the edge of her coffee cup, leaned over the table with one hand on her hip and said, "I realize that insanity runs in the Lawson family, Bennet, but I had hoped you would be spared."

Rats, Bennet thought, falling heavily into his chair as his mom spread a little more of Aunt Suzy's orange marmalade on her English muffin. She had not taken her eyes from Bennet. She was waiting. Bennet hated when she waited like that. It put him all on edge. Why couldn't she be more like Harve's mother, Mary Margaret—who, Bennet and Harve were convinced, had never had a secret emotion or an unexpressed thought. Not his mom. She just sat there with her ears and nose twitching, like a cross between a rabbit and a satellite dish. She just sat there in silence, decoding Bennet's secret signals and waiting for him to confess.

"I don't guess I'm really terminal," Bennet said, pushing his Cheerios to the bottom of the bowl with his spoon and watching them bob back up to the top.

"Good," his mom said. There was a long silence, while Bennet played with his cereal and his mom waited.

Mercifully, the phone rang.

"I'll get it," Bennet shouted as he and Fred ran for the phone. "Hello. Hello, Mrs. Melton. Yes, ma'am. Just a minute . . . Mom!!!! It's for you."

His mom rose and walked confidently to the phone. "Hi, Mary Margaret. What's up? You're kidding? I don't believe it. Not again. No, that's no bother at all. It's on our way. Tell Harve that Bennet and I will blow the horn for him at a quarter to eight. Sure. No problem. Talk to you later. Bye."

Rats, Bennet thought.

His mom moved to clear the dishes from the table. "Mary Margaret asked us to stop by and pick up Harve on the way to vacation Bible school. Big Harve left for a sales meeting in Crenshaw County and took both sets of keys again. She's fit to be tied. I don't know if she was more upset because she can't go anywhere or because Harve offered to hot-wire the car for her." His mom paused. "He can't, can he?"

"Oh, Mom!" Bennet said, putting his head in his hands.

Bennet's mom was rinsing and stacking the dishes now. With her back to Bennet, she asked, "Well, Bennet, do you think you want to go, or should I call Mrs. Fletcher and see if she can stay with you?"

Mrs. Fletcher, Bennet thought, his head still in his hands. The commandant.

"I guess I'll go," he said, without conviction, as he headed to his room to get his rainbow-colored King Jesus fanny pack with the half-finished

Campbell's soup can shakshuka he'd been working on in crafts. He shook the can filled with pebbles. Boy, those Israelites were sure hard up for music before God invented electricity, he thought, as he stuffed the can, his asthma spray, and a couple of Spider Man comic books in the pouch and attached it around his waist.

Bennet's mom knocked on his door and stuck her head in. "Ready?" she asked cheerily.

Bennet gave her that flatlined-mouth look that he tried to copy from Charlie Brown and followed her in silence to the car. He didn't even say good-bye to Fred.

What a difference a day can make, Bennet thought as they turned down College Street for the short drive to Woodland Circle, where the Meltons lived. Yesterday morning Bennet had leapt into the car. As a matter of fact, he had been so excited that he had jumped from the car the very second it pulled up to the curb and had made the bend and curve of the sidewalk to the church at Olympic-qualifying speed—so much so that while running through the swinging doors of the church with such speed and force he had run, unseeing, right into the ample thighs of Mrs. Lindemann, the vacation Bible school's music director, and had caused them both to lose balance and crash onto the plush carpet floor.

Mrs. Lindemann took it pretty well. Mr. Branson from the bank—who had been dropping off his teenage daughter, Florence, one of the teaching assistants—had nearly had a stroke, though.

"He has had nightmares about liability from an early age," Florence explained.

Mrs. Lindemann just sat there like a splat of English garden in her floral-knit dress and laughed until the tears fell down her face. After all, she said, she was well padded. Mrs. Lindemann was of the school of thought that the more jelly donuts consumed at a single sitting, the greater the operatic range.

"Bennet Boling Lawson," Mrs. Lindemann said, still sprawled on the carpet. Bennet, who had scrambled to his feet in horror, could only keep repeating, "I'm sorry. I'm so sorry," over and over again.

"Bennet Boling Lawson, we could have used you in Desert Storm and saved a bunch of money on tanks."

By this time a small crowd had gathered. Mr. Branson, Florence, and Reverend Tucker managed to raise Mrs. Lindemann to her feet again.

Mr. Branson turned to Bennet. "Bennet, what is the matter with you?

Don't you know better than to run around like a Tasmanian devil in the house of the Lord?"

"Oh, leave the boy alone, Chuck," Mrs. Lindemann said. "He wasn't trying to kill me, for heaven's sake. Lighten up. Do you want him to think that God's house is just a place for boring, long faces— where he can never be himself or make a mistake?"

Reverend Tucker, seeing that Bennet was close to tears, put her arm around him, making his humiliation complete.

"I sure am sorry, Mrs. Lindemann," Bennet said. "It won't happen again."

"No harm done, Bennet. I wish I had a little of your energy," Mrs. Lindemann said, smoothing her dress over her hips. "Go on in the sanctuary and relax. We'll be starting the music soon."

Bennet walked down the center aisle slowly and deliberately, like a bride, and sat down on the third row with Harve and the other boys, who were giggling and snickering without mercy.

That had only been the beginning. Mrs. Lindemann, thinking she was showing no hard feelings, had put monotone Bennet in the front row of the choir and called on him to sing a solo line in "Father Abraham."

"Why don't you try to emphasize the motions a little more next time, honey?" she said, her eyebrows raised in horror after Bennet had given it his best shot.

At snack time, he and Harve had been arm wrestling on the corner of the snack table, and Bennet had fallen into the orange drink and had to sit on a plastic garbage sack in the fireside room for story time. Then, to top it all off, during recreation, he had wheezed so badly during the Ark of the Covenant Relay Race that Reverend Tucker had pulled him aside, put a halo on his head, and made him a heavenly judge.

All this passed through Bennet's mind as Laura made the winding turns up Woodland Circle and pulled up to the curve in front of the Meltons. Two blasts on the horn brought Harve running from the house. Mary Margaret came out on the front porch with a cellular phone in one hand, alternately waving, making key motions, and pointing to the phone with her free hand.

The morning went fairly uneventfully, until Florence Branson began to divide the group up for recreation. Bennet knew this was the day for the First Annual "Festivals of Jesus" Olympic Games, with sack races, spoon hanging, golden trumpet blowing, and "Score One for the Skipper" volleyball competitions.

*Bennet: Stories of Humor, Grace, and Hope*

While Florence had her back turned, getting the smaller children off to their games of Pin the Sword on Judah and the vacation Bible school's version of Duck, Duck, Goose—Esther, Esther, Mordecai—Bennet slipped behind the curtain.

Reverend Tucker had watched this from the rear of the sanctuary, but she decided to wait to investigate until the others had left the building. Just when Bennet was beginning to think he had gotten away with it, the curtain swept back and there stood Reverend Tucker in her "Ladies Sewing Circle and Terrorist Society" T-shirt, cutoff blue jeans, and "John Calvin Was Right" baseball cap. Reverend Tucker was a woman of contradictions, but Bennet liked her.

Without a word, Reverend Tucker dropped down cross-legged on the floor next to Bennet. "How's it going, Bennet?" she asked.

"Fine," Bennet replied.

"Good. Good," Reverend Tucker said, playing with the rim of her baseball hat. "So, Bennet, did you lose something back here?"

"No, ma'am," Bennet said.

"Good. Good." There was a long pause. Sometimes Reverend Tucker reminded Bennet of his mom. "So, you just kind of thought you might hang out back here in the dark for a while, I guess."

"I thought I might," Bennet said, hopefully.

"Good. Good." Long pause. "How come?"

"I guess I don't like recreation time too much," Bennet answered.

"Oh," Reverend Tucker said. "Don't you like to play with the other children?"

"Well," Bennet risked. "I like it sometimes, but nobody ever wants me to be on their team."

"Oh," Reverend Tucker said quietly.

"I don't breathe so good sometimes," Bennet offered.

"Oh," Reverend Tucker replied.

"Yesterday Florence had to make the Angelic Host team take me. I was picked dead last, even after Evelyn Cartwright, who always wets her pants."

"Oh."

"It was an awkward moment," Bennet said.

"I'll bet it kind of hurt, too, didn't it? Made you wanted to kind of show them all, huh?" Reverend Tucker said.

"Yeah. I showed them all right. You had to pull me out of the game."

"I'm sorry about that, Bennet. I didn't do it to embarrass you. You know it's not because the other kids don't like you, don't you, Bennet?"

"I know," Bennet said, not looking at her. "Sometimes I just want to be like everybody else."

"Yeah," Reverend Tucker said. "People have never been too good with things or people who are different, have they, Bennet?"

"Guess not," Bennet said.

"It's just like what happened in the early church," Reverend Tucker said.

While Bennet was wondering what had happened at the eight o'clock service that he hadn't heard about, Reverend Tucker startled him with a question.

"Bennet, do you know what faith is?"

"Sure," he said, hoping she wouldn't ask him what.

"What?" she asked.

Rats, Bennet thought. "Faith, uh. It's kind of like what you believe, isn't it?" he said.

"Yeah. It kind of is. In the Bible, it says that faith is the assurance of things hoped for, the conviction of things not seen."

Bennet was confused. That was the expression Bennet's Uncle Ralph in Chicago used whenever Bennet's mom asked him what he thought the chances were of the Cubbies making it to the Series.

Before Bennet could ask, Reverend Tucker continued. "The assurance of things hoped for means that God will make good on God's promises. Do you know what God has promised you, Bennet?"

Bennet tried to think if the angel Gabriel or the old, dead prophet Jeremiah had mentioned that when they came to visit Bennet when he was sick. He couldn't remember.

"Does it have anything to do with me having a baby?" Bennet asked.

Reverend Tucker looked puzzled. "I really don't think so, Bennet. The first Christians thought that God had promised them a land and offspring, but I don't think you have to worry about having a baby. The point really was that they believed God had promised the very best for them. God promised that they would be secure and have the things they needed to be happy and safe. Most of all, God promised that they would always be chosen first on God's team—God would be our coach and also our best friend, and nothing that happens can ever change that. Does that make sense, Bennet? Faith means *knowing* that God's promise is true and *living* as if it is real for you.

---

*Bennet: Stories of Humor, Grace, and Hope*

Bennet thought about this for a moment. He could almost see himself running to the head of the line as God, in a long white robe and baseball cap with the word "coach" in big letters on the front, giving him some last-minute advice before the big game. Bennet smiled. Reverend Tucker watched for a moment, then continued.

"The conviction of things not seen means that God is bigger than what happens to us. God is bigger than what we see and feel. Because God is so big and powerful, and because we matter so much to God, we can hold on when things are really bad. We can reach for God's hand when we hurt or when we are scared—that hand will be there, and that power. When we do that, we can reach beyond our limits. It doesn't mean that our limits will go away. It just means that we have the power to rise above them."

Bennet thought he understood this, too. He remembered once when he was in the hospital in an oxygen tent and the doctor had to cut down into his ankles to find veins for the IVs. Bennet remembered his nurse holding his hand and saying, "Reach, Bennet. Reach down deep and breathe, Bennet. You can do it, Bennet. You'll see. Everything will be okay."

Bennet told this story to Reverend Tucker. Her voice got a little husky for a minute, and she cleared her throat several times before she said, "That's right, Bennet. That's exactly right. Faith means believing that God will make good on God's promises one of these old days, and letting that knowledge make you strong."

Suddenly, something strange happened. Suddenly, the little room behind the dossal curtain lost its musty smell. It was filled with a silver light and the scent of healing herbs, just like when the angel Gabriel came to Bennet to remind him how much God loved him. In the silver light, Bennet could see himself on a beautiful playground in the middle of a meadow filled with wildflowers. He could feel his lungs expand and fill with air. It was as if he was actually there, running and jumping and throwing a ball hard.

As Bennet wheezed out that deep breath, he knew it was real—that meadow and those lungs. He knew that God had dreamed him whole and promised that he would get there—someday, somewhere. He would get there. Until then, he would unwrap God's gift of faith every day.

And he would wait.

And he would reach.

# 6

# Bennet and the Fitful Night

Once upon a time in a land far away, somewhere to the South and a little to the East, a small boy named Bennet lay awake one night trying to conjure up a sore throat so he wouldn't have to go to school.

"Rats," he said, swallowing hard and feeling no pain. His Chihuahua dog, Fred, was dreaming loudly by his knee. It was one of those wonderful spring midnights, when the land smelled of fresh rain and the moonlight danced on point through the flowering trees, leaving patterns of Swan Lake or Giselle on the quilt Bennet's grandmother had made for him.

Bennet usually slept like a rock, and he usually liked school. Recently things had changed: "recently" being yesterday during recess. Keith Adams—the biggest and best-looking boy in his class, and the one who had gotten to play the part of the lead shepherd in last year's church Christmas pageant after Bennet got sick on Christmas Eve—had brought his new kitten, Tompkins, to school for show and tell. Unbeknownst to Bennet, Keith had sold tickets for a quarter to everyone in the third and fourth grades who wanted to watch Bennet blow up with an asthma attack when Keith threw the kitten in Bennet's face at recess.

Now the fact that Keith had done this dastardly deed was not the bad part. The fact that Keith Adams was a jerk had been previously established. The bad part was realizing that over half the school had been willing to give up their lunch money to this jerk just for a chance to see Bennet swell up, turn red, and choke.

Mary Catherine Conrad—who had spent most of the last year crying behind the willow tree during recess because her mother and father were getting a divorce and her father and older brother were moving away—had put a stop to the scheduled debacle by telling the teacher.

Keith had had to give everybody's money back, but the damage was done as far as Bennet was concerned. He had spent the rest of the day going over every face in the room, trying to decide who had bought in. Everyone denied it, but Keith Adams had a fruit jar with about seventy-five quarters in it. "So, you do the math," Bennet had said to his best friend, Harve Melton, who had tried to comfort him at lunchtime.

Bennet was humiliated. Furthermore his teacher had called his mother, Laura, at work and told her the whole grizzly tale. His mother had "given birth to about fifteen chickens on the living room floor" when she got home from work. She was on the phone demanding a PTA meeting, public apologies, and a mandatory health class that dealt with pulmonary disease.

It was your basic nightmare. At nine o'clock, when Harve had called to tell him that most of the class was grounded, that nobody would speak to Mary Catherine, and that Keith's father was talking military school, Bennet knew he could never go back.

"Rats," he said again, swallowing hard. "Well, Fred," Bennet said. The little dog lifted his head and raised his ears into semaphore position. "Well, Fred. We'll just have to run away," Bennet said quietly, slipping out of bed. He dragged the small, blue duffel bag, which was kept partially packed for swift trips to the hospital, out from under his bed. He dressed warmly, stuffed a few more items in the bag, and headed for the kitchen to put some food in a baggie for Fred.

"You stay, Fred," Bennet said, as the dog jumped off the bed and followed him to the kitchen. Within minutes Bennet was packed, Fred was on his leash and they were out the door and down the street.

Bennet didn't know what time it was, but the street was dark and quiet. Every now and then he would hear a dog bark in the distance and Fred would freeze like a statue and turn his head from side to side, deciphering.

They had gone a few blocks when it occurred to Bennet that he needed

---

*Bennet and the Fitful Night*                                                    37

a plan. He'd have to go pretty far not to be in the same school, like all the way out of the county. He wasn't quite sure which county that was. Maybe he could hop on a freight train and jump off in Fort Deposit, which he knew was in the next county. No. His mom would come for him there. Maybe he should get on the bus and try to look up Mary Catherine's father and brother.

Thinking about Mary Catherine made Bennet sad. She had stuck her neck out for him and now none of the other kids would talk to her. Harve said that Mary Catherine's mother had called his mother crying, saying that Elizabeth Hamilton had called and uninvited Mary Catherine to her spend-the-night party the next Friday night and that somebody had rolled their yard.

Bennet was passing the brick fence that rimmed Miss Sarah's Williamsburg cottage, out on the edge of Mountain Dale Street, when he decided to stop and sit on the fence to think.

Bennet knew Miss Sarah. She was eighty-four years old and a devout Episcopalian. She had her own prayer chapel, with holy water and everything, built right into her house. Bennet liked her, so did his mom, so did everybody, except Father Craven, the local priest who never turned the chalice or polished his shoes to suit her. She had threatened for years to join the Presbyterian church where Bennet and his mom went, but when the church had called Reverend Tucker—Reverend Marilyn Tucker—right out of seminary and six months pregnant, that had been the end of that.

Miss Sarah always came to the Presbyterian choir concerts and put her three-legged dog, Rachel, in the church's annual dog show. She always took a special interest in Bennet because her oldest son, Charles, had died from a severe asthma attack when he was seven.

As he sat on the wall in front of Miss Sarah's house in the dark, Bennet thought about all these things, and Mary Catherine and Memphis, and whether the fumes of the Greyhound bus would make him sneeze.

Suddenly, the porch light flashed on. Bennet and Fred jumped and turned to face Miss Sarah, who was holding a walking stick in one hand. Three-legged Rachel was growling behind her left foot.

"Bennet Lawson? Is that you?" the old lady asked.

"Yes, ma'am," Bennet replied.

"Lord, have mercy," she said. "What in the world are you and that dog of yours doing on my fence at one o'clock in the morning?"

"We were just . . ."

"Get in this house! Your mother must be out of her mind!"

Bennet hung his head and dragged Fred behind him up on the porch. He had not believed that things could get worse, and they just had.

As he walked into Miss Sarah's house, the smell of old Oriental rugs and furniture polish swept over him.

"Have a seat," she said, pointing to the dimly lit parlor with her cane. "Now!" Miss Sarah said, and waited.

For a moment Bennet thought he could outwait her, but when he glanced up and was caught by her watery, blue eyes fixed on his face, he knew he couldn't.

"Well, Miss Sarah, Fred and I were thinking of heading up to see Mary Catherine's father and brother for a while."

The old woman never blinked as the whole story came tumbling out of him—all about Tompkins the kitten, and Keith Adams, and half the class buying in, his mom pitching a fit, Mr. Adams talking military school, and poor Mary Catherine being uninvited to Elizabeth's house, and how, all in all, he thought he and Fred "might just leave."

"I see," Miss Sarah said. "And what about Mary Catherine?"

Bennet was stumped. "What about Mary Catherine?"

"Are you just going to leave and let Mary Catherine pay the price for what happened?"

"Well," Bennet said. "I thought I would."

"I see," the old woman said. "Where is your faith, Bennet?"

Bennet couldn't remember where he put it, so he wrinkled his brow and said nothing.

"Let me tell you a story, Bennet," the old woman said, settling back in her chair with the white lace doilies on the arm. "Bennet, a long time ago in a place called Philippi, which was a Roman province not too far from Damascus, Paul and his friend Silas . . . do you remember them?"

Bennet remembered Paul because of how Reverend Tucker would sometimes get red in the face when the subject of Paul came up. He didn't remember Silas. "Yes, ma'am," Bennet answered.

Miss Sarah continued. "Paul and Silas were in Philippi telling people about Jesus. One day they ran across a little slave girl who was being led around by her owners on a rope. Everywhere they went, people paid money to hear her tell prophecies. Over and over, when she saw Paul and Silas, she would say, 'These men are slaves of the Most High God, and they come to offer a way of salvation.' Well, this made Paul and Silas furious because in their day that was like saying they worshiped a God who was just one among many and that this way of salvation was just one among many. Do you see why this was a problem, Bennet?"

"Yes, ma'am," Bennet said, although he had never thought about it before and wasn't quite sure why he was being called on to think about it in the middle of the night, in Miss Sarah's parlor, with Fred trembling in his lap and Rachel growling at his feet.

Miss Sarah continued. "Well, finally it got out of hand and Paul and Silas had to put a stop to it. They said that a demon was causing her to do this, and in the name of Jesus they cast it out of her. Her owners were furious because they couldn't make money from the slave girl's problem anymore. They trumped up some police charges against Paul and Silas, accusing them of disturbing the peace, not being registered citizens, and not following the religious laws. Paul and Silas were beaten and put in jail."

"They were pretty upset, but there was nothing they could do about it. They just sat up late and prayed and sang together. Well, lo and behold, about midnight," she leaned forward in her chair, like she was telling a ghost story around a camp fire. "Lo and behold, about midnight, God sent an earthquake. It broke down the walls of the prison. Paul and Silas could have escaped, but they didn't. They waited until morning."

When the prison guard woke up, he was going to kill himself because he thought they had escaped, but he was stopped by them. They told him about Jesus, and he and his whole family became believers. See?"

Bennet sat there for a moment, imagining that long-ago scene and wondering what it could possibly have to do with Mary Catherine.

"Bennet," the old woman sighed. "Do you understand what I am trying to tell you?"

Bennet sat looking into her blue eyes. "No, ma'am," he said.

She sighed again. "Bennet, what happened yesterday was a lot like what happened to that slave girl. Someone who did not have your best interest at heart, Keith Adams—who would, in my opinion, much benefit from military school, except that the idea of him knowing how to use a weapon is a frightening prospect—sought to make a profit at your expense. Like Paul did in his day, Mary Catherine did what had to be done to stop it and to stop people from thinking that what Keith did was all right. Now she may not have known exactly what she was doing, but basically she was not going to allow something to go on that was damaging to you and could damage others if they came to believe it was all right. What did she get for her trouble? She got cut off from her friends and from the activities she enjoyed and had planned on. A little like getting thrown in jail, isn't it?" She waited for Bennet to reply.

"Yes, ma'am," Bennet said, amazed. It was the first time he could identify a positive attribute of a girl, and he was startled.

"Bennet Boling Lawson," the old lady said. "I believe that God may be calling you to be an earthquake."

Suddenly, when the old woman said his full name, he felt that the room was filled with a bright silver light and with the scent of healing herbs, like it had been the night the angel Gabriel came to him, like the night that old dead Jeremiah showed up at the foot of his bed, smelling like a goat and telling him that God wanted him to be a prophet. He had told Jeremiah about Mary Catherine that night, as he recalled, but nothing much had come of it.

"Angels come in the ways they can be received," Gabriel had told him. As Bennet looked through the sparkling silver light at the old woman and the three-legged dog, he realized that this, too, was an angelic visitation, a message from God just for him.

"How can I be an earthquake, Miss Sarah?" Bennet asked with his eyes wide and his nose twitching from the smell of the herbs.

"Well, Bennet, I'm not sure. What the earthquake did for Paul and Silas was let them know God could release them from their bondage. The earthquake let them know that the worst things people do would never hold them down in the end. Do you think you might find a way to be an earthquake for a little girl whose father just moved away and who the most popular girl in school just uninvited to a spend-the-night party?"

"I could maybe call her and tell her thank you," Bennet offered feebly.

"You could maybe tell her in person in the morning at school."

Bennet gulped.

"In front of Keith," the old woman added.

I knew I was going to hate this prophet stuff, Bennet thought. Be nice to a girl, in front of Keith Adams. Bennet just shook his head.

Miss Sarah, noticing the shake of the head, leaned back in her chair and closed her eyes. "Who knows, Bennet Boling Lawson." Bennet drew up all his strength at the sound of his name. "Who knows, Bennet Boling Lawson. Maybe, like the jailer, Keith needs an earthquake, too."

The room was silent for a moment, except for Fred and Rachel, snoring. Bennet could hear the clock in the courthouse tower strike two. The moonlight flooded in the window and seemed to cover the old woman in gauze that looked like the angels' wings the little girls wore in the Christmas pageant. Bennet was suddenly very sleepy.

"Well, Bennet. It's time to go." The old woman got up, took some keys from the hook by the door, and headed toward the carport door. Bennet followed a few steps behind, carrying Fred perched on his duffel bag across his chest. Miss Sarah backed the huge, old Buick out of the drive.

"If we're going on a trip, we need gas," she said.

Bennet could see her blue eyes sparkle in the dark.

"Maybe I have a few things I need to tend to first, Miss Sarah."

"Maybe so," Miss Sarah said as they turned down Mountain Dale for home.

# 7

# Bennet and the Chocolate Angel

Once upon a time in a land far away, somewhere to the South and a little to the East, a small boy named Bennet hid under his grandmother's quilt on a cold December morning, plotting his revenge. The object of this revenge was Harold Carmichael, the meanest boy in school. Harold Carmichael always picked on everybody. Well, not exactly everybody—just the easy targets like Mary Catherine Conrad, who was insecure and used to hide behind the willow tree and cry during play period until she moved to Memphis with her mother after her parents' divorce.

Without Mary Catherine, Harold had spent the fall casting about for a new target. More times than not, it was Bennet. Most of the other kids had made their peace with Bennet's asthma, and most of the time so had Bennet, but not Harold. Every time Bennet wheezed while playing kick ball, or when some poor, unsuspecting substitute teacher showed up wearing perfume, it was like waving a red flag in front of a bull for Harold. He would snort and carry on, clutch his hands to his chest, roll his eyes back in his head, and say such totally obnoxious things as, "Oh, Miss Scarlett, where are my smelling salts?"

Bennet had taken to watching the Greyhound bus stop in the afternoons after school, hoping that some scrawny kid with chicken-pox scars from Chicago or some such place would move to town and take the heat off him for a while.

"The time is at hand, Harold Carmichael," Bennet murmured, paraphrasing Reverend Tucker's Sunday sermon, and punching the quilt with his prophet finger. Bennet had been enthralled with Reverend Tucker's sermon last week on John the Baptist in the wilderness. Bennet could identify with weird old John racing around in the wilderness in smelly clothes, yelling at anybody that came near him to repent. All week Bennet had been feeling called by God to make sure that Harold Carmichael mended his wicked ways—dead or alive.

This is the day, Bennet thought, rolling over and unsettling his Chihuahua dog, Fred, who had been snoring loudly under the covers. Bennet could hear his mother, Laura, moving around the bathroom, running water, dropping cosmetic jar lids in the sink. He knew it was only a matter of time before she would stick her head into his room and say, "Up and at 'em, Bennet." What an obnoxious thing for a person to say first thing in the morning to somebody they claim to love.

His mother stuck her head in, "Up and at 'em, Bennet."

"Rats," Bennet mumbled, sticking his head out from under the quilt as Fred jumped off the bed and scampered after his mother to the kitchen. As Bennet threw his legs over the side of the bed, he saw the neatly ironed white shirt and blue pants that his mother had hung out for him on the mantle piece.

"Double rats," he said, remembering this was the day that the music teacher, Mrs. Sandi Appleby, who looked just like her name, was taking his class out to the Camellia Glade Nursing Home to sing "Rudolph, the Red-Nosed Reindeer," "Silver Bells," and "Frosty, the Snow Man" to all the old people.

Bennet couldn't sing a lick, not a lick. So he got to provide the "physical interpretations," as Mrs. Appleby called them. What that meant was that he got to wear reindeer antlers and gallop on a broom in front of the other kids while they sang "Rudolph." He got to shake gongless bells during "Silver Bells," and melt like the wicked witch of the West for "Frosty, the Snow Man."

It was the first time Bennet was glad that Mary Catherine Conrad had moved to Memphis. At least she would not have to witness his hour of humiliation. Harold would be there, though.

"Triple rats," Bennet said, as he stuck his feet into his slippers and scuffed across the hardwood floors to the bathroom.

The bus ride to the Camellia Glade Nursing Home was a successful experiment in chaos. The only good thing was that Ruth Mendelson threw up, and that kept Harold Carmichael occupied. Mrs. Appleby was as excited as if she was opening in *Cats* on Broadway. She had even bought a long-stem red rose for one of the children to present to her after the final bows.

As the bus pulled into the parking lot, Mrs. Appleby flushed red and said, "Children, for an encore, I think we should do the "Twelve Days of Christmas." You remember all the motions, don't you, Bennet?"

Suddenly, Bennet understood why Ruth Mendelson had thrown up. He could feel Harold's beady eyes fixed to the back of his head. It was a good thing Harold wasn't very smart, so Bennet could be out of the bus and headed for the door before Harold could think of anything revolting to say.

The performance went about as Bennet had expected. Harold pinched all the girls and made them squeal and lose their places, while Bennet stood on one foot and peered through a pecan branch twelve times, pretending to be a partridge in a pear tree.

Mercifully, it ended, and Bennet had the opportunity to slink to the back of the crowd while Mrs. Appleby took her bows. She waved her red rose and curtsied to the old people, like she was meeting the Queen.

"Now, children," Mrs. Appleby said, flushed with triumph. "We have about half an hour for you to visit with the residents before we go back to the school."

Bennet didn't hear the rest of what she said. He was already down the hall, hoping against hope to duck into a room, any room, before Harold spotted him. He dove toward the first open door he came to and found himself standing before an old man in a wheelchair with a bright tartan blanket over his lap.

It was Old Smoke Robinette. Bennet had seen his picture in the paper a bunch of times. He was the oldest man in the county, 103, and got his picture in the paper every year on his birthday. Old Smoke was the color of a three-year-old Hershey bar, deep chocolate brown covered over with a fine white mist. He had been an engineer for the Rock Island Railroad out of Des Moines for years, but he had come home to die. That was thirty years ago, after the diabetes took both of his legs at the knees. Old Smoke was still bright as he ever was, though, which everybody in the county knew was brighter than everyone else in the county.

Bennet was wondering if Old Smoke was blind, so maybe he could sneak back out of the room without being seen.

"Who are you?" Old Smoke snapped.

"I'm Bennet Lawson, sir," Bennet said. "Ho! Ho! Ho!"

"Come here, boy," Old Smoke said, motioning with a hand that looked for all the world like the ghost of Christmas-yet-to-come. Bennet inched forward. "You Sammy Lawson's boy?"

Bennet had never even heard of Sammy Lawson. "No, sir. My dad's name was Fred, but he's been gone a long time. My mom's name is Laura. She was a Boling and works over at Thigpen's Drugstore."

"Oh, that new place," Old Smoke said.

"Yes, siree," Bennet said, remembering all the overtime his mother had put in last summer for Thigpen's Twenty-fifth Anniversary Sale.

"Have a seat," the old man said, motioning Bennet toward the bed. Bennet perched uncomfortably and waited. "You one of them kids that was singing?"

"Well," Bennet said. "Actually, I did the 'dramatic interpretation.' "

"Can't sing, huh?" the old man said.

"Not a lick," Bennet responded.

"Me neither," the old man said, clapping a watery eye on Bennet's face. "What'd you bring me?"

"Well, uh," Bennet stumbled.

"Well, I hope it isn't none of that soggy divinity candy like last year."

"Well, actually, we didn't actually bring any gifts . . . yet."

"Speak up, boy. You got any candy or not?"

"No, sir."

"Humph. Can't sing. Ain't got no candy. Don't know your pappy. You're a poor excuse for a Christmas elf."

"Well, uh, actually, I just stopped by for a minute to say 'Ho! Ho! Ho!' " Bennet knew he wasn't supposed to say Merry Christmas the first week of Advent, because it made Reverend Tucker question her call. Bennet's mother always put up their tiny Christmas tree the first weekend of December. Ever since Reverend Tucker came to the church, they had kept a small daisy afghan next to it. Bennet had been carefully instructed to throw the afghan over the tree if he saw Reverend Tucker coming up the walk before the third Sunday in Advent. Reverend Tucker and the entire church had actually made their peace with Advent years ago. The parish pretended to listen to her, and she pretended to believe that they did. It was a workable arrangement for everybody.

The old man was silent. "Ho!" Bennet said once more. The old man never took his eyes off of him. "Actually . . . actually," Bennet said, looking at his hands. "Actually, I'm sort of hiding out."

"Aha!" the old man said. "Now we're getting somewhere. Who's after you, boy? Are they armed?"

Before he knew what was happening the whole grizzly story poured out in that raw voice that passes for childhood rage and indignation. Bennet told him all about how, since Mary Catherine had moved to Memphis, Harold always pretended to swoon and faint whenever Bennet had an asthma attack, and how he had started calling him "snow-cone nose" in honor of his *Frosty* performance. How, in one of the great mysteries of the universe, the name had stuck. Now, everyone called him that, including most of the girls who never called him anything at all. He told him all about how he thought he was the new John the Baptist, and how it was his duty to make everybody, especially Harold, repent. When he had finished, he and the old man sat in silence for a moment.

"You ready for Christmas, Bennet?" Old Smoke asked.

Bennet didn't know what he had expected, but it wasn't that. "I guess so," Bennet said, embarrassed now that he had told the old man anything.

"Baby Jesus is going to have a hard time findin' you," he said. Bennet, who had in the last year been visited personally by the angel Gabriel in the form of a donkey with wings for ears and by the prophet Jeremiah in a smelly woolen coat, found it hard to believe that there was not a detailed map to his house hung up on the refrigerator in heaven.

"I haven't moved, sir," Bennet said.

"That's the truth," the old man said. "And it's time you do. Jesus'll never get to you with all that dead brush you got inside of you. It ain't no wonder. Your daddy's gone. Your lungs ain't so good. You're that dumb Carmichael boy's kicking post. Your girlfriend moved away. You can't sing. Your insides are all covered over with brush. You got to get it cleared before Christmas, or Jesus'll get lost in there and never find you."

"She's not my girlfriend," Bennet said. He could feel the tears balling up in his throat. That was all he needed: to get back on the bus with his eyes looking like Rudolph's nose.

---

"Well, whoever she is, she done moved to Memphis and left you hiding out in my room."

Bennet lowered his head. The ball of tears in his throat was twisting and turning and threatening to leak, and he decided that the only way to deal with it was to pout.

"You know, a person's insides are just like a jungle, Bennet," the old man continued. "Things get all overgrown and tangled up. Inside jungles grow on the moisture from pent-up tears. When we let the tears out, the jungle don't grow up so fast. Does that make any sense to you, boy?" Old Smoke asked.

Bennet swallowed hard and nodded. "I don't have much experience in the jungle," he said. He had gone to the tropical rain forest at the zoo in Birmingham once with his cousins, and he had sneezed for two whole days after. He didn't think jungles were healthy places to explore.

"What did the rest of that Bible verse you were quoting off of your preacher say? Do you remember?"

"No, sir," Bennet said.

"Well, first it says 'Repent,' which, by the way wouldn't hurt you either, but we'll get back to that. It says make a straight path for God. Do you know what that means?"

"Clear the jungle?" Bennet ventured unsure.

"That's exactly right, Bennet. Clear out all that stuff that you've thrown up to hide you from God. All that stuff that's inside of there," he said, punching at Bennet's chest with the cane he used to push the TV on and off. "All that stuff you hide in."

Bennet thought about that for a minute. "But I don't know how, Mr. Robinette," the young boy said.

"Well, Bennet, you'll have to teach your own self. We all do, but I'll just bet you might find the place to start right back there at 'repent'. Maybe you should start there."

"Me?" Bennet interrupted. "But I haven't done anything!"

"You ain't?" Old Smoke asked and waited.

Bennet scanned his brain. For the life of him, he couldn't come up with a thing. He shook his head.

"Well, maybe you ain't as notorious a sinner as that Carmichael boy, but it does seem to me that you been lying to God for a while."

Bennet was insulted. "I have not! I never lied to anybody," Bennet said, reaching for his nose to see if it had grown.

"You ain't happened to tell God that everything'd be pretty much okay, if a pox just happened to fall on Harold Carmichael?"

"Well, maybe I did mention it once," Bennet said, remembering the schemes he wove under his grandmother's quilt that very morning. "But what if I did? It's the truth."

"No it ain't. Harold didn't cause you to have asthma. Harold didn't run off your daddy. Harold didn't load that little Conrad girl up and drive her to Memphis. Harold ain't much of the problem. Do you know what the problem is, Bennet?"

Bennet thought about all this. Harold wasn't the problem? Well, if he wasn't, what was? Suddenly it was as if the old man's room was filled with a silver light, and Bennet could feel his nose tingle at the scent of healing herbs. He knew that Gabriel was right close by. Bennet remembered Jeremiah telling him that Gabriel would always be close by, only a little farther away than God.

"But what is the problem?" the small boy asked the old man.

"The problem is that you believe him, Bennet. When Harold says those mean things about you, you believe that they are true. And no matter how hard God tries to tell you otherwise, the first voice you hear on the subject of *you* is Harold. Bennet, when you put God second, in any way at all, even in who you listen to, that's a sin. Every time you catch yourself doing it, you need to apologize to God and start over. That's how you start to clear the jungle. That's a way to start making a straight path for God. That's how you let the baby Jesus find you on Christmas."

"I wish I could sing," Bennet said, "and that I could breathe a little better, and that Mary Catherine hadn't moved away, and that I knew my dad." The tears began to fall down his cheeks. The old man didn't say a word, but reached over his hand—or hoof, Bennet couldn't be sure—and brushed away the tear so there would be room for the next.

After a few moments the old man said, "Bennet, are you going to have a Christmas tree, you and your mama?"

"Yes, sir," Bennet said, not mentioning that it had been up almost a week already.

"Well, boy, when you look at that tree, you think of it as the first brush cut out of your jungle. You hang it all full of colored lights and pearly balls. You thank God for the courage to cut it down—and the fact that because it's cut down now and all decorated with light and joy, it can't no longer block Jesus' way to you. You thank God that you've made the straight path one step closer to your heart."

Bennet jumped up from the bed and leapt at the old man, scaring them both. As he threw his arms around the old man's neck, he thought he heard the sound of tinkling bells, like the bells Gabriel wore on his collar when he came to visit Bennet last Christmas Eve.

"Thank you, Mr. Smoke," Bennet said.

"Ho! Ho! Ho!" said the old angel.

# 8

# Bennet and the Holy Way

Once upon a time in a land far away, somewhere to the South and a little to the East, a small boy named Bennet hid behind the kitchen door and listened to his mother on the telephone.

"Mary Margaret? Laura. Hi. How are you doing? Well, I guess I'm okay. Well, to tell you the truth, I'm a little worried about Bennet. I know that I'm probably overreacting, but last night, when Bennet showed me his Christmas list, it didn't have on it any of the things he'd talked about all year. As a matter of fact, right at the top of the list, marked with three stars and 'Early Delivery Requested', was a Barbie doll with wedding dress and trousseau. You're kidding? Harve, too? Well, I just don't understand it. There's nothing wrong with it, I suppose. When I asked him about it, he just said he was striking a blow against sex-role stereotypes, ran out to the backyard, and threw rocks at squirrels for half an hour."

Rats, Bennet thought. He had hoped his mom and Mrs. Melton would be too embarrassed to compare notes. It would make things much more difficult if they ganged up.

"Did you ask Harve?" Bennet's mom questioned. "Well, what did he say?" She laughed.

Bennet knew what his best friend Harve had said, because he had called him the night before to commiserate. Harve had told him that his parents had put the screws to him. He finally said that he figured a Barbie doll was the closest he'd ever get to a girl, with his buckteeth and freckles. That had not seemed to comfort his mother, who was the nervous type. He had heard his father on the phone later, signing him up for karate lessons at Beeland Recreation Center.

What their parents didn't know was that Bennet and Harve were on a mission from God.

It had all started last Thursday evening, when Bennet was sitting cross-legged on his bed, reading his latest Spider Man comic book with his little Chihuahua dog, Fred, dressed up in a Batman cape and ears, snoring loudly beside him. Bennet was deeply engrossed in the triumph of justice, when he heard the front doorbell ring and his mother sprint from the kitchen to answer it.

Bennet peeked through his cracked door to see his mother greet Chuck Branson, the bank president and the chair of the church's corporate committee.

"I won't take up much of your time this evening, Laura," Chuck said, after waving away her offer of a cup of coffee with a flip of his hand. "I know you have to get to choir practice. Laura, I just stopped by to ask you to see if you can talk some sense into Marilyn. She listens to you."

Marilyn was Reverend Tucker and the bane of Chuck Branson's existence, as had been every minister at the First Presbyterian Church since the Korean War. Bennet was really interested now.

"Chuck, what in the world has got you in such a dither now?" Bennet's mother asked, motioning Mr. Branson to have a seat on the couch. They sat.

"I suppose you've heard about that family of gypsies that is camped out over at the RV park?" the bank president asked.

"I don't recall," Bennet's mother lied. Actually, she and her women's group had discussed the situation in detail the day before. Sue Sheffield, the sheriff's wife, had said that her husband had come home in a foul humor the night before. Chuck had read him the riot act when he reported, after investigation, that it was not a family of gypsies after all. It was a young Mennonite couple and their children from Indiana, who were making their way south in search of work and a place to call home.

"Well, apparently these people set up camp about a week ago," Mr. Branson continued. "Blew in after that last snowstorm up north, I guess.

Anyway, who knows how many more will come if we have a mild winter. Now don't get me wrong; I don't have anything against these people personally. I'm just worried about our children and the effect this thing might have on the town. First thing you know, we'll be just like New York City: Children will be begging on the street corners, squirting dirty water on your windshields when you stop at a light, and then expecting you to pay them to wipe it off."

"Well, if that's the case, maybe they'll bring some decent theater with them when they come," Bennet's mother said, trying unsuccessfully to hide her irritation with humor. "Besides, Chuck, it's a public park, isn't it?"

Mr. Branson sat in silence. After an interminable time, Bennet's mother continued. "And where does Marilyn fit into this?"

"Well, you know how she is. All I asked her to do was call the other pastors in town and try to schedule a public meeting at the church to discuss the problem. She all but called me Scrooge and suggested that if I wanted them out of the park, I should offer them our carriage house."

Bennet's mother covered her grin with a cough. "I'll discuss it with her, Chuck," she said, making a mental note to ask Marilyn after choir practice about the possibility of a Giving Tree for the children.

"Thank you, Laura. You're a sensible woman," Mr. Branson said, rising from the sofa and heading for the door.

Bennet quietly closed his bedroom door. "Did you hear that, Fred?" The little dog raised his ears. "Gypsies! Cool!"

Just at that moment, Bennet felt a small vibration in the floor, like the old wood had shuddered and stretched.

Earthquake! he thought, and dove under his bed and waited. Fred had settled himself back on his blanket, and Bennet could hear his mom moving coat hangers around in her closet. He waited. Nothing. After a respectable period of time, Bennet crawled out from under the bed and looked around. The room was filled with a silver light, and the scent of healing herbs tickled his nose. He noticed a small point of light by the ceiling fan. As he watched, it began to spin and grow. First, it was the size of a pinhead, then a rhinestone, then a dime, then a quarter.

"Is that you, Gabriel?" Bennet asked. The light had stopped spinning now and was about the size of the palm of Bennet's hand. He could see now that it wasn't a light at all, but a snowflake.

Bennet had never actually seen a real snowflake. He knew that's what it was because Mrs. Killough, the history teacher, grew up in Buffalo, New

York. Every December she cut snowflakes out of white tissue paper and taped them to the windows of her room, where they stayed until the sun caused the points to curl.

"No," the snowflake said.

"What?" Bennet said, startled. Bennet thought that in the last year he had seen it all: The angel Gabriel had come to him in the form of a donkey with wings for ears; the prophet Jeremiah had shown up smelling like an old goat; and the pond at the monkey house at Beeland Park had frozen over, and people had gotten out their ice skates and skated on it. Now a talking snowflake was in his room. Bennet quietly accepted his fate. There was nothing to be done but become eccentric.

"No," the snowflake said again.

"No what?" Bennet asked.

"No. I'm not Gabriel."

"Oh," Bennet said.

"My name is Isaiah," the snowflake said.

"Well, no wonder nobody listened to you," Bennet said. "No offense or anything."

"None taken, my boy. None taken. Besides, I wasn't a snowflake in the old days. Although there were those who thought I was a little flaky. Ha! Ha!" The snowflake pulsated when it laughed. "I just came to you as a snowflake to get your attention. The Boss knows you have a flare for the dramatic. Now, down to business: The Boss has an assignment for you."

"I don't suppose we're talking Springsteen?" Bennet said glumly, thinking of the records his mother turned up loud while she was working in the garden.

"Who?" the snowflake asked.

"Never mind," Bennet said. "What's the gig?"

"God wants you to remind the Welches about what I said."

"Who are the Welches, and which part of what you said?"

"The Welches are the family Mr. Branson was telling your mother about, the folk out at the RV park. God is worried that they are losing hope and they need a little boost."

"Don't they have a Bible?" Bennet asked, hoping to get out of this assignment before the snowflake figured out that he didn't have a clue about one single word Isaiah ever said.

"They do have a Bible, and they read it, but the words have become old to them. They don't seem real anymore. When I said all that stuff about sorrow and sighing fleeing away, barrenness blooming, the exhausted being energized, and the helpless receiving power, I was talking to exiled people—to what you would call homeless people—nearly thirty centuries ago. The Welches don't think those words apply to them anymore. God wants you to find a way to tell them that they do."

"Maybe I should write some of this down," Bennet said, heading for his desk.

"You don't need to write it down, Bennet. It's not my words that matter. What matters is that everything I said had to do with helping people find home again. All I really said was that the power of God's love for us in the Messiah—you call him Jesus—the power of God's love for us in Jesus gives us a highway home. Remember when I said there shall be a highway there, and it shall be called the Holy Way? That's what I meant. Jesus gives us a highway home to God. Jesus gives us a happy future no matter what happens now or what has happened before. That's what God wants you to tell the Welches."

Bennet thought about the time he had gone up to Camp Tuckabatchee for a week to experience nature. It was a beautiful place with lots of trails, streams, and a big lake nestled in the foothills of the Smoky Mountains. Bennet had loved it, except at night. At night, when he crawled into his bedroll, he missed his mom, Fred, the way the pipes creaked in the old house, and the sound of the sprinkler cooling down the roof on a late summer afternoon. At night, when it was dark, Bennet wanted to go home. He thought about the family sleeping in the dark at the RV park.

"They're homesick," Bennet said to the snowflake.

"On earth we all are, Bennet. It's just that some of us are safe, living in hope, and that makes the longing bearable, even joyful; others feel only the pain and fear."

"But why me?" Bennet asked.

"Because you understand," the snowflake said and was gone.

Bennet's mother knocked on his door and stuck her head in to find Bennet standing in the middle of the floor, staring at the ceiling fan.

"What are you doing, Bennet?" she asked.

"Thinking about camp," Bennet said. "Is it time to go?"

His mom nodded and Bennet grabbed his coat, patted Fred, and followed her to the car. Bennet and his best friend, Harve, always went with their parents to choir practice. They sat in the back pew of the church, plotting and scheming, while the organist tried to find a way to play this week's anthem around the keys that were either stuck or silent.

Bennet told Harve the whole story. Well, the whole story except for the part about the snowflake. Bennet knew that all friendships had their limits. He told Harve about Mr. Branson coming to the house, about the little family, and how it was their duty to do something.

The next afternoon they rode their bicycles out to the RV park, hid behind a camellia bush, and watched the little family. The father wasn't around, and the smell of kerosene threatened to blow their cover as Bennet held back a sneeze. The little girl seemed a year or so younger than Bennet. She was sitting on a camp stool by the door of the tent. One arm was in a cast and the other held a rope, which was tied around the waist of a toddler who was wearing a too-small romper and gathering and playing with sticks. The little girl was looking through a ragged magazine. The mother was washing out diapers in a big tub. On a bush by the water spigot, they had tied pictures from the magazine to the branches with pieces of string. Bennet and Harve could see pictures of festive meals, houses lit with twinkling lights, and a Barbie doll in a long white wedding dress.

"Go talk to them," Harve said.

"You go talk to them," Bennet whispered.

"You go. It was your idea."

"It was not," Bennet said.

"Then whose idea was it?" Harve asked.

"I don't want to talk about it," Bennet said. The young girl looked up from her magazine and stared at the camellia bush. She opened her mouth to call her mother, and Bennet and Harve took off.

By the time they breathlessly reached Bennet's driveway, the idea of the Barbie dolls had been formed and sealed with a secret oath. Bennet and Harve never betrayed each other. They were too highly evolved.

Now Bennet was hiding behind the kitchen door, listening to his mother's worried voice bemoaning the lack of a father's steady influence in Bennet's life.

I'll never hear the end of this, Bennet thought, as his mom hung up the phone, picked up her garden clippers, and headed to the backyard to clip some camellias for the coffee table.

Bennet made a dash for his room. All week long he had been gathering trinkets and hiding them in a checked tablecloth under his bed. He had a paper cup filled with cheese straws, a stack of Spider Man comic books, a couple of toy trucks, and some tinsel.

*Bennet: Stories of Humor, Grace, and Hope*

"Pitiful," he said, banging his head on the slats of the bed as he inspected his trove. He added the beaded Indian headband that he had made at Camp Tuckabatchee. After much deliberation and not a few tears, he added the crèche that he had received for Christmas the year before. The inspection complete, he tied the tablecloth together at the corners, shoved it under his pillow, and waited.

As soon as his mother was asleep, he would make his move. Bennet had been out alone at night only once before—the time he tried to run away from home—and he was nervous about it. As soon as the house was dark and quiet, Bennet crept from his bed, shushed Fred, put on his coat, and grabbed the tablecloth. Slowly, he raised the old window and unlocked the screen. He tossed the sack of gifts to the ground and lowered himself after it.

The street was empty, except for his next-door neighbor, Frances, and her fullback boyfriend. They didn't notice him. Suddenly, Bennet saw the snowflake again. It was just ahead of him and seemed to light a tiny path for him to follow, like a long-ago star.

When he got to the RV park, all was quiet, except for the sound of the father snoring restlessly. Bennet crept soundlessly to the front of the tent and dropped the sack, taking a moment to pin the note he had carefully written earlier with the help of the snowflake. "The Holy Way leads to the Holy place," it said, "with love for the journey home."

Bennet slept soundly that night, and he didn't dream. He was still sound asleep, when his mother knocked on his door and stuck her head in the next morning.

"Up and at 'em, Bennet," she said.

"Oh, God," Bennet mumbled, sticking his head under the pillow. Selfless charity takes a lot out of a person.

"Bennet, I'm going over to the church to help Marilyn take the gifts we gathered out to that poor family at the RV park. Do you want to go?"

Bennet popped up. The gifts? What gifts? "Yes, ma'am," he said.

"Well, hurry up. We've got to get a move on it. Maybe we can go to the Pancake House for breakfast after. Would you like that?"

"Sure," Bennet said, digging through his drawer for a clean sweatshirt.

As soon as Bennet, his mom, and Reverend Tucker turned the corner to the RV park, he knew the family was gone.

"Well, I just don't understand it," Reverend Tucker said, making the loop of the park twice. "I guess they just moved on, poor things. They must have left early this morning, because they were still here yesterday, according to Chuck."

They pulled up next to the small pond and stopped the car. "May I get out for a minute?" Bennet asked.

"Do you have the time, Marilyn?" Bennet's mother asked.

"Sure, Bennet, but just for a few minutes."

Bennet jumped out of the car and headed to the sight where the young family had been. The kerosene smell was still strong, but the sight was neatly cleaned—not a trace, except one. On the bush where the pictures had hung was tied a small slip of paper. "Thank you, signed Julie Ann," it said.

Bennet picked it up and turned it over. "Thank you," it said on the back. "Signed, the Snowflake."

# 9

# Bennet and the Positive ID

Once upon a time in a land far away, somewhere to the South and a little to the East, Christmas morning dawned cold. A small boy named Bennet was wiping ants off the window sill and believing more in the Grinch than in Santa Claus. Bennet curled his lip and imagined himself stuffing some silly toy marked Cindy Lou in a knapsack and heading for New Orleans.

Bennet was feeling put upon. The whole Advent and Christmas season had been different this year. Your basic experiment in terror—the children's music program at the Camellia Glade Nursing Home—had been a nightmare. Harold Carmichael would never let him live down that "Partridge in a Pear Tree" thing. Then Bennet had snuck into the closet where his mother hid his presents, only to discover that she really had gotten him a Barbie doll like he asked for, and the poor little homeless girl he had wanted it for was probably camped out somewhere around Tampa by now.

Furthermore, Bennet thought his mother should be wiping off the ants. After all, she was the one who had sprinkled the powdered sugar on all of the windowsills, in front of the front door, and even by the chimney before they had left last night for Christmas Eve service. Bennet could hear her now merrily humming over the turkey as she squeezed the bird's juices with a basting bulb over its fat, tanning breast. She was acting as if nothing had happened.

His mother's purse had been stolen from a counter at Maden's department store the morning of Christmas Eve. She became convinced that the thief would come and wipe them out while they were at church. Lewis Sheffield, the sheriff, had promised to have one of his boys drive by every fifteen minutes, all night long. Bennet's mother had not been comforted. A person could stuff a lot of silver flatware in a book bag in fifteen minutes.

After the outrage over the loss of her driver's license, credit cards, and Bennet's baby pictures had subsided somewhat, a steely calm had settled over his mother. When she looked at Bennet, she looked like a pine tree in an ice storm, assaulted and covered over with a sheet of crystal.

"Well," she had said, as they ate their grilled cheese sandwiches and tomato soup at the kitchen table after Lewis and his assistant had left. "Well, Bennet, if that thief thinks he can make off with our Christmas, he's got another thing coming. If he comes into our home, we'll get him," she said, leaping from the table and grabbing the box of powdered sugar, which still sat open on the counter from the orgy of bay point cakes his mother had made for her gift baskets.

Bennet munched quietly on his sandwich as he watched his mom sprinkle the powdered sugar on the windowsills. "We'll get his fingerprints, or at least his sorry footprint, if he tries to come in here."

Bennet watched in resignation. While he had never witnessed it personally, ever since he had seen the picture of his mother sliding down the fire pole in her bikini in her high-school yearbook, Bennet had known that his steady, Rock-of-Gibraltar mother was capable of erratic behavior.

Bennet could hear her moving through the living room, muttering to herself, "Think you can steal our Christmas. Ha!"

This was a new thought for Bennet. Until that moment, it had never occurred to him that Christmas was a thing that could be stolen, like a microwave oven. Was it really that God came to us in the boxes wrapped under the tree? Was it possible for someone to steal God? Could something that another person did take Jesus away? Could God get so ticked off that the cradle really would remain empty this year? any year? ever?

"What is Christmas, anyway?" Bennet pondered, as he heard his mother head into her bedroom.

"Bennet," she called. "You better get ready for church. The Meltons will be here to pick us up in half an hour, so we can help put out the luminaria."

Bennet had decided to ask Reverend Tucker about all this when he got to the church. When he saw her, though, she had that off-in-the-ozone, communing-with-the-angels look on her face, and Bennet knew he didn't have the flight gear to reach her.

"Rats," he said, as he poured kitty litter into the small paper sacks for the luminaria.

"What's that, Bennet?" asked his best friend, Harve, who was following behind Bennet, dripping small candles onto the mounds of kitty litter with sounds of the Luftwaffer.

"Nothing," Bennet said.

After the service, Bennet, his mom, and the Meltons always went over to Mandi Nicholson's for tree trimming and eggnog. Mandi grew up Catholic in New England, and she never put her tree up until Christmas Eve. It wasn't so much for religious reasons anymore—after all, she was a Methodist now—but to maintain her adored foreign status.

Bennet's mother was nervous about being away from the house too long, so Harve's father took a swing by to check things out on the way to Mandi's. All was quiet, and she saw one of the sheriff's cars making the turn down the side street just ahead of them and was comforted.

Mandi was an antique dealer, and she was the only person in town to live in a blue New England saltbox house. She had come to town from Massachusetts, after her husband died. The little house was crammed to the gills with things—antiques she had bought for the shop and couldn't bear to part with, pictures, magazines, books, and box after box of tissue-wrapped ornaments, all of which had to be carefully placed on her annual three-foot coffee-table tree.

It was a ritual that everybody loved. Mandi greeted them at the door in a turban and a flowing print gown that looked like a bathrobe. Both were festive, but they only accentuated the effects of the surgery and chemotherapy. As Bennet dove toward a bald spot on the tree with the paper-mâchè pelican he always chose to put on first, he again wondered if there would be Christmas without the pelican and the widow Nicholson.

The thought passed quickly as Harve nudged his hand from the tree and hung his icicle on the very branch Bennet had spotted for the pelican. After the predictable tussles, the nutmeggy eggnog, and the annual family stories, all bade goodnight to Mrs. Nicholson, piled into the Melton station wagon, and drove the few blocks home.

"Good night, everybody. Merry Christmas!" Bennet's mother called, as she and Bennet climbed the front steps arm in arm and the Meltons pulled out of the driveway.

When they entered the house, Bennet's mom had a moment of renewed vigilance. She glanced at the floor and windows. No sign that the sugar had been disturbed. "Safe and sound," she announced. Then she packed Bennet off to bed and went to prepare the ingredients for the turkey stuffing.

Bennet was momentarily distracted by the mounds of presents under the tree. He sent up a secret prayer, "Please don't let them all be Barbie clothes." His mom had to shoo him into his room with her brand-new handbag.

As soon as he closed the door, he saw the woman. She was standing in the corner by his desk with her hands folded in front of her. She was thirty-something, not very tall, with dark black hair pulled back in a bun at the base of her neck. She was wearing a trench coat with the collar turned up and a black felt hat that seemed to hum and beep a little.

"Whoa," Bennet said, jumping back against the door.

"Bennet Boling Lawson," the woman said, before Bennet could gather his wits. "I have a message for you."

Oh, no, Bennet thought. It wasn't enough for God to send donkeys, prophets, and snowflakes to talk to him. Now he had to send somebody's mother.

The woman began to walk toward Bennet.

"Are you an angel?" Bennet asked, trying to see if there was a bulge underneath the trench coat that might be wings folded down.

"No, Bennet," the woman said. "I'm not an angel. I'm just a friend from a long time ago. My name is Priscilla."

"Oh," Bennet said, relieved. "You're Elvis's wife." Bennet hoped that maybe God had finally answered his prayers for singing lessons.

"Not *that* Priscilla, I'm afraid, Bennet. My husband's name was Aquila. We had a small business in Corinth."

Bennet looked at the woman carefully. She was very calm, and her gaze at Bennet was steady. Bennet began to sweat.

"Bennet," she said. "I may as well get right to the point. God is worried about you and asked me to come for a visit and help you with your search. You can think of me as a sort of cosmic female Columbo."

Bennet was amazed—a ghost detective.

"What search?" Bennet asked.

"Why, Bennet, your search for Christmas, of course."

Bennet was silent for a moment. "So it really is lost," Bennet said glumly. "I just knew it."

"Well, maybe not lost," the woman said. "Maybe it just needs to be uncovered for you. Maybe you've forgotten how to look for the clues. That's why God sent me to you."

Priscilla moved toward Bennet's desk and sat down. "Let's get to work," she said, motioning Bennet to be seated on the foot of his bed. "Now, how shall we go about finding Christmas?"

Bennet thought.

"Think like a detective, Bennet," she said hopefully.

Bennet thought some more. Nothing.

"Well," she finally said. "What if we start by describing what it is we're looking for. What is Christmas, Bennet? How would you describe it?"

"Well, Christmas is Jesus' birthday party. It's when everybody spends all their money, gets the flu, exchanges presents, and eats too much."

The ghost detective laughed, "Okay, so Christmas is a birthday party that sometimes gets a little out of hand. Who is this Jesus and why do we want to throw him a party?"

"Well, he was this little kid that was born in a manger a long time ago. His mother had been riding on a donkey, and they couldn't find a hotel room because some kind of convention was in town and his dad forgot to call ahead. After he was born, everybody—angels, kings, and stuff—sang all over him, and they gave him presents because they felt bad about the manger and all. Then, he grew up, turned into God's son, made everybody mad, got executed, was raised from the dead, and disappeared."

The woman looked at Bennet with her clear gaze. "I think you may have tangled up a few of the facts there, Bennet, but we'll deal with that during your next hunt. What's important now is that you remember that this Jesus we throw the party for is—and by the way, he always was—God's son."

"Well, you know," Bennet burst in. "I think Joseph was a really good sport about the whole thing. My friend, Harve, and I were discussing that very thing, just the other day." Bennet and Harve had indeed held that discussion while hiding in Harve's basement, watching soap operas on his grandmother's old TV. Disgusted with some young starlet's torrent of tears,

Bennet had turned to Harve and said, "People certainly get worked up about paternity, don't they?" And so the subject was broached.

"You're right, Bennet. Joseph was a really good sport about it all. You see, with a little help from God, he was able to understand how important it was for all of us that Jesus be God's son. Do you know why that is so important, Bennet?"

Bennet didn't have a clue. All Bennet remembered was that Harold Carmichael had made Tom Wilbanks, the youth minister intern from the seminary, cry during Sunday school the day he was trying to teach them about the Trinity. Harold Carmichael showed no mercy to anybody.

"Was it because God needed somebody to take to games? Or did he need somebody to take over the family business someday?" Bennet suggested hopefully.

"Bennet, I know that this is hard to grasp. You see, Bennet, it is important that Jesus is God's son because we needed somebody who could help us see God. At least, that's one reason. We needed a human being who could get through to us a little better about who God is. See, angels and prophets just didn't seem to be as believable to people as a real live son. People for so long had been looking for God. Jesus was just the clue that they were looking for. He was like God's fingerprint. When people identified Jesus, they had a positive ID on God. Everywhere that Jesus went and everything that Jesus did were clues as to what God is like—and what God is up to. Whenever people see Jesus, they see God's own fingerprint."

"You know what makes me mad?" Bennet said with energy. "What makes me mad is that I don't ever see Jesus. All over the world, we throw this big party every year for him and he never shows up, unless he shows up in New York City or someplace. What good is a fingerprint if it's invisible?"

"That's a good question, Bennet," the woman answered, pushing a strand of unruly hair back from her forehead. "Jesus is not visible to you, as he was to the shepherds and kings so long ago, but Jesus is still present. You can find him in the stories of the Bible for one thing. If those seem to get a little stale to you sometimes, Jesus has left his fingerprints all over the place, too. They are not completely perfect prints, like Jesus' print of God. They are partial prints, enough that if you look hard you can make a match."

Bennet glanced at the windowsills to see if the sugar had been disturbed. No signs.

"Where are Jesus' fingerprints?" Bennet asked.

"They are all over the place, Bennet. You just have to train yourself to see them. That's a big part of what being a Christian is all about—being a detective for God, training yourself to see the clues that point to God's presence in the world, training yourself to find the fingerprints of Jesus all around you."

This sounded a little too much like work to Bennet. "Can you show me the first one?" Bennet asked.

"Okay, Bennet," the woman said, rising from her seat. She walked slowly to the center of the room, lifted up one hand and pressed the air, like she was leaving her handprint on a sidewalk in Hollywood. When she removed her hand, there it was, caught in the light of the bedroom and spinning as if on a tiny thread. There it was, a perfect fingerprint, like a tree ornament crafted in the finest crystal and polished to a high sheen.

"Wow," Bennet said. He reached up to grab the fingerprint, but it was gone. "What happened to it?" Bennet asked in distress.

"You don't need it anymore, Bennet. It is printed on your heart now. You will never forget it. For the rest of your life, whenever you see that print, you will recognize it."

Suddenly, the room was filled with a silver light, and the scent of healing herbs tickled Bennet's nose. The woman pulled the collar of her coat farther up her neck, touched her finger to the point of Bennet's nose, and was gone. Bennet sat and tried to look at the tip of his nose for a few minutes, then got ready for bed.

As soon as he had awakened, Bennet had pounced from bed and begun a careful search of the house. There was not a fingerprint to be found. Nowhere. Nothing probably but Barbie dolls he'd have to try to flush down the toilet before Harve came over.

As he wiped more ants away, Bennet heard his mom humming in the kitchen, just as she had last night. "How's it going, Bennet?" she called. "Charlotte, Hugh, and the kids will be pulling up any minute."

"Bah, humbug," Bennet mumbled.

Bennet heard a car door slam and looked up. His mother's sister and her family had arrived. The station wagon was rocking from the impact in the driveway. Bennet's cousins, Ginny and Lloyd, had tumbled from the car and were chasing each other around the magnolia tree. Charlotte and Hugh were rummaging in the trunk.

Bennet gasped.

Ginny and Lloyd were heading for the front door, but Bennet couldn't see their faces plainly. They were covered with a labyrinth of fine gray lines.

"Fingerprints," Bennet whispered in awe. As he turned to call his mom, the room began to swirl. It was filled with fingerprints—on the packages under the tree, on his Chihuahua dog, Fred, on the box of cookies that his mother's friend JoAnn had made.

His mom walked from the kitchen, wiping her hands on her apron. She had a big, smudged fingerprint, just over her left eye.

"Mom," Bennet said, the tears rolling down his nose, but not affecting the fingerprint. "Mom, it's Christmas!"

# 10

# Bennet and the Sign

Once upon a time in a land far away, somewhere to the South and a little to the East, a small boy named Bennet was sitting in about a foot of water at the edge of Turkey Creek, squishing red mud through his toes and mumbling under his breath.

"Rats," Bennet said out loud as he looked at the other children just a few feet away, hovering intently over a picnic table. It was the last day of asthma camp at Camp Tuckahoo, and Bennet was in a foul mood.

For three years he had badgered his mother, Laura, to allow him to go to Camp Tuckahoo. Finally, she had given in. It had been everything Bennet had dreamed. He had skinned his knee, won a ribbon in a relay race, short-sheeted a counselor's bed, and met little Carolyn Whitehead. She was from Nashville and wore a little oxygen tank on her back. Bennet thought she looked like a Rocketeer princess, especially in her yellow two-piece bathing suit with the ruffles on the top and bottom. She had jumped and cheered when Bennet won the relay. Even the fact that this sight had caused Bennet to stumble into the trophy table had not marred the sacred moment.

Now it was over. After the picnic lunch, parents would begin to stream in past the timber poles that marked the camp entrance, gather up their mosquito-bitten, triumphant children, and head home.

Bennet loved his home, but somehow the ordinariness of it seemed shabby today. He didn't want to go back there. Nobody would understand. Harve would ask how it went and then not listen when he told him. His mom would tuck him in at night and say the same bedtime prayer, just as if nothing had happened. He'd go to school and be the last one chosen for teams, just like he'd never won a blue ribbon in his life.

Bennet made his mouth a straight line. "Rats, rats, rats," Bennet said, squishing the mud between his toes with each word. The mud rose up in the water in little swirls, turning the green to copper before it settled back to the bottom. Bennet was watching the mud settle, when suddenly the water around his feet began to make an eddy. As the little whirlpool grew wider and wider, so did Bennet's eyes.

As Bennet watched, he saw what looked like feathers emerging from the center of the whirlpool. At first, they just lay on the water like the sails of a downed clipper. Then they seemed to organize, and a large pair of nostrils rose from the whirlpool, sniffing and sputtering.

"Gabriel? Is that you?" Bennet asked as the donkey's head rose from the water, twisting and flapping the wing-ears to dry them off.

"At your service," the angel answered, rising from the water and sitting next to Bennet as if he were sitting in an easy chair. He had all four legs stretched out in front of him, and one wing over Bennet's head for shade.

"Long time, no see," Bennet said. Bennet had not seen the angel Gabriel—who often appeared to him in the form of a donkey with wings for ears and feathers for a coat—since last Easter, although he had often felt the angel's presence nearby.

"Well," Gabriel said, twitching his nose and pointing it toward the sun. "I've been keeping an eye on you." They sat in silence for a moment, then the angel continued, "How've you liked camp, Bennet?"

"It's been pretty cool," Bennet said, not looking at him.

"Why aren't you over there with the other children, then?"

"Oh, they're just making a dumb sign," Bennet replied.

"What kind of sign?"

"Just a sign to hang up for when the parents get here. It's supposed to say, 'Welcome to Camp Tuckahoo.' Then, everybody is supposed to draw their favorite thing from camp and then explain it to their parents, when they get here."

*Bennet: Stories of Humor, Grace, and Hope*

"That sounds like a pretty neat thing to do," the angel offered.

"I think it's dumb," Bennet said, kicking the water and watching the mud fly.

"Why, Bennet?"

"What good does a dumb sign do anyway? Camp's over."

"I see," the angel said, scratching his chin with a hoof and flaring his nostrils. Bennet kicked the water again. "Bennet, all sign making is an act of hope." Bennet rolled his eyes and then stared expressionlessly at the angel.

The angel continued, "Bennet, do you know who Joshua was in the Bible?"

Bennet thought for a minute. He knew he'd heard of him and he tried to remember what Reverend Tucker had said about him. "Joshua, Joshua," he murmured. "Was he the guy with the talking donkey?"

The angel grinned. "No, Bennet, that was Balaam." For a moment the angel got a faraway look in his huge brown eyes. "That was a fun one," he said.

"That was you!" Bennet said.

"Of course, Bennet. How many of us do you think there are?"

Bennet had given this no thought. "I guess I just kind of thought I was the only one you came to like this."

"Oh, no, Bennet. God is all the time going to extraordinary measures to get through to somebody."

Bennet did not know if he was comforted or disappointed. "Oh," he said.

The angel looked at him and waited. Then he prodded, "Now, about Joshua."

"Oh, yeah," Bennet said.

"Joshua," the angel continued. "Joshua was the one who led the people of Israel into the promised land after Moses died. Do you remember now?"

Bennet almost remembered.

"Anyway," Gabriel continued. "After their long journey and all the things they had gone through trying to get there—all the hardships in the wilderness, the internal squabbles, the miracles, the hard, hard work, Moses up and dying—after they finally got across the river Jordan, Joshua made everybody stop. He sent some of the leaders to get some stones out of the river Jordan. He told them to set the stones up to be a sign, so that when their children asked what the stones meant, they could tell them all about what

---

God had done for them on their journey home." The angel waited.

Bennet stuck his lower lip out. The angel stuck a hoof under the water and into the red mud, flipping out a small, smooth stone and tossing it into Bennet's lap. It landed with a splash. "So, Bennet, what's God done for you at Camp Tuckahoo?"

Bennet fingered the stone and rinsed it in the water. "Well, I suppose God kept me well," Bennet said.

"I suppose God did," Gabriel said.

"And . . . and . . . I can't really think of anything else."

"Let's go after it this way, Bennet. What has been most special to you about camp?"

"Well," Bennet said, "I won a blue ribbon in a relay race on Thursday. That was way cool. I never won anything like that before, I mean, a normal prize, like for running around. I never even got to run the relays at school because of my asthma and all, but it was different here. Everybody could run. Kids ran with their oxygen packs. That was great. Everybody ran and got a chance." The angel nodded, and the small boy continued. "I learned a whole bunch of new stuff I never knew before—about plants and stuff, about what the names of the plants mean and about all the animals that live up here and how to take better care of them. I mean, I knew some stuff before, but it was like there was a whole new layer of things that I never thought about before. We did all kinds of fun things as a group. We worked as teams, sat around the camp fire, had special meals, sang songs, and laughed a lot."

Bennet took a breath, and Gabriel nodded again. After a moment, he said, "I made a bunch of new friends." He was thinking of Mike from Fort Payne, who had been his canoe partner, and Charlie from Tuscaloosa, who had known all the ghost stories, and Carolyn, who had cheered for him and looked the other way when he ran into the trophy table. His eyes began to fill with tears. "I want it to last forever," he said, leaning on the donkey's withers while its wing-ear curled around the boy's shoulder.

"I know," the angel said. "This is a hard thing you're having to do, Bennet. God knows how hard it is to do. That's why God sent me here to talk to you. God was worried that maybe there were a couple of things you didn't realize that might help you."

Bennet didn't look up.

"First of all, God has provided you with all these experiences, just like God has always provided for the people. God thought long and hard about how much you needed to feel like a winner, how you needed to be part of a team, how you needed to celebrate, make mistakes, and overcome them. That's why God brought you here. Everything has happened for a reason. Do you know what the main reason is?" Bennet shook his head. "The main reason is so that you could understand the kind of life that God wants you to live. God wants you to have celebrations and victories. God wants you to learn what is behind the surface of things, and how to have friends who are there for you. Bennet, that kind of life is possible—not just at Camp Tuckahoo, but everywhere—because now you know what to look for. Camp Tuckahoo never ends, because you carry the experiences, celebrations, and the things you learned with you wherever you go."

"But what about the people?" Bennet asked.

"Well, Bennet, that is the hardest part, saying good-bye to the people who have shared this week with you. That will hurt, because you and I both know it won't ever be just the same again. God wanted me to tell you something very important about good-byes. Bennet, Christians never have to say good-bye for the last time. Maybe you will get together on other occasions, meet at camp next year, or go away to the same college. Maybe you will not meet again in this life. Bennet, God knows what a treasured gift friends are, and they will never be taken from you forever."

Bennet thought of his friend William, who had died just before Easter and all the things Reverend Tucker said about life in the presence of God. The angel tucked the small boy under his wing and held him there for a moment, then was gone. Bennet had not felt him leave. He had smelled the scent of healing herbs, though, and felt the way the silver light the angel always left behind touched his skin.

"Bennet," a voice said from behind his shoulder. Bennet whirled around to see Carolyn standing with a paper plate of chocolate cake and melting ice cream.

"Don't you want some cake?" the little girl asked shyly.

"Thanks, Carolyn," Bennet said, standing up and wiping his muddy hands on his already-muddy bathing suit.

"We saved a spot for you to put something on the sign," she said, as they headed to the table.

"I think I'll draw a rock," Bennet said.

"Why?" she asked.

Bennet told her all the wonderful things he had told Gabriel. Well, all except about her yellow two-piece bathing suit.

"It's been a cool week, huh?" she said.

"Yeah," said Bennet. "It's been a cool week."